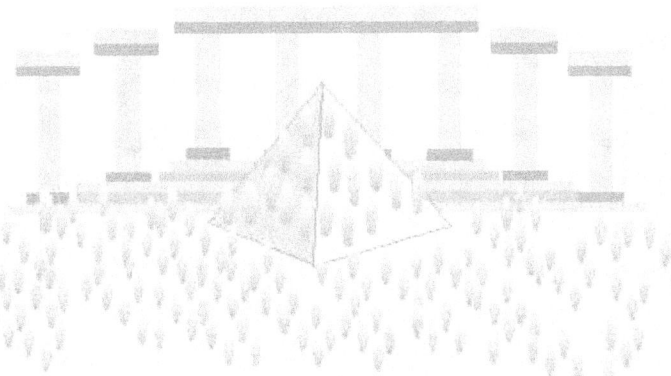

The coliseum-like structure resembled ancient Roman architecture except for the large pyramid rising up majestically in the center. Various groups of entities were interspersed around the base of the pyramid, casually interacting with others around them.

Suddenly, as a sprinkling of soft musical notes enveloped them, each and every personality stopped and waited expectantly. Within moments, an impressively illuminated group of "Speakers", as they were called because of their superior wealth of knowledge and experience, appeared on one of the uppermost rims of the pyramid. The majestically hypnotizing music intermingled with the non-verbal interchange that followed between the Speakers and the various groups.

"Matters are progressing well, Electra."

"Yes...I was pleased that we were able to perceive a mental glimpse tonight of the interrelated futures in our current physical states."

"Soon your soulmate will be seeking your advice and knowledge in this realm when he finds himself here after his physical termination..."

First Edition April, 2003; reprint 2005

ISBN: 978-0-9794585-0-7

Printed in the U. S. A.

SOUL
SURVIVOR

By

Jolinda Pizzirani

www.SummerlandPublishing.com

To Patrizio, Christian and Stefania --
the most wonderful family I could wish for --
thank you for all of your love and support.

To Helen, my soulmate, who
began this journey with me.

And to all my wonderful friends
and relatives who have encouraged
these writings.

PREFACE

The coliseum-like structure resembled ancient Roman architecture except for the large pyramid rising majestically from the center, various groups of entities were gathered around the base of the Pyramid, casually greeting others around them.

As a sprinkling of soft music enveloped them, every personality stopped and waited expectantly. Within moments, an impressively illuminated group of 'Speakers', so called because of their superior wealth of knowledge and experience, appeared on one of the uppermost rims of the pyramid. The hypnotic music intermingled with the non-verbal exchange that followed between the Speaker and the various groups.

Rosamond listened intently as specific questions were asked by the Speakers. She felt well prepared to answer anything they might ask before finalizing her rebirth into the physical state.

She glanced quickly at an adjacent group for a communication with Electra, her soulmate. In their last physical coexistence, they had been brothers in World War 1. As planned. they both had sacrificed their lives during the war. Now, they wanted to return as husband and wife, although not meeting until late in life so they could accomplish the many other lessons they had each decided to undertake.

As Rosamond was receiving a fleetingly swift "thought" message from Electra. the Speakers interceded abruptly.

"HAVING QUITE SUCCESSFULLY COMPLETED FIVE PHYSICAL EXISTENCES, ROSAMOND, YOU HAVE REQUESTED AN ADDITIONAL, FINAL EXPERIENCE IN THE THREE-DIMENSIONAL REALM, CORRECT?"

"YES, THAT IS TRUE." Rosamond answered somberly. *"I UNDERSTAND THAT I WOULD NORMALLY BE ADVANCING TO THE NEXT REALM, HAVING ACHIEVED THIS LEVEL OF*

UNDERSTANDING AND UNIVERSAL KNOWLEDGE.   HOWEVER, IT IS ALSO CUSTOMARY TO ALLOW ONE AN 'OPTIONAL'... OR.. 'EXTRA' PHYSICAL EXISTENCE IF SO DESIRED, IS IT NOT?"

"A CUSTOM RARELY PRACTICED, TO BE SURE," the Speakers conceded. *"HOWEVER, IN A CASE SUCH AS YOURS WHERE EXTRAORDINARY CIRCUMSTANCES EXIST -- AND CONSIDERING YOUR ABUNDANT WILLINGNESS TO BE OF ASSISTANCE..."*

Rosamond took the chance to interrupt politely. *"IT IS KNOWN WHAT MUST BE ACCOMPLISHED IN THE NEXT TIME-SPACE IN ORDER FOR THE CURRENT PHYSICAL REALITY TO SURVIVE, AND MORE IMPORTANTLY, TO 'PROGRESS'. I FEEL CAPABLE OF PERFORMING TO YOUR SATISFACTION."* She hesitated, then added quietly, *"EVEN WITHOUT THE BENEFIT OF MY BANK OF ACCUMULATED UNIVERSAL KNOWLEDGE."*

The Speakers quickly confirmed their decision amongst themselves, then announced, *"IT WILL BE AS YOU REQUEST."*

Rosamond threw a quick spurt of happiness in Electra's direction.

"HOWEVER..."

Rosamond's attention was immediately returned to the Speakers as they reminded her forcefully, *"DO NOT FORGET THAT YOU ARE FAR BEYOND ELECTRA IN HER LEVELS, AND WILL THEREFORE BE EXPECTED TO ACT ACCORDINGLY IN THIS, YOUR FINAL COEXISTENCE ON EARTH TOGETHER, BEFORE YOUR ADVANCEMENT."*

"I UNDERSTAND," Rosamond said solemnly.

The Speakers now turned to direct their words to all those present around them.

"WHILE IN THE PHYSICAL STATE, YOU WILL ALL CONTINUE TO RECEIVE CONSTANT SUPERVISION AND ASSISTANCE THROUGH YOUR MANY SUBCONSCIOUS DOORS TO THIS REALM." They paused, then said simultaneously in thought-voices which rang over the groups below louder and clearer than any physical sound in existence. "BE ONE. ONE WITH EACH OTHER, THOSE YOU WILL ENCOUNTER, AND ALL THAT IS."

As the tremendous reverberation gradually faded, the Speakers slowly dissipated and floated into nothingness, leaving their distinct imprint on the minds and personalities of each of those remaining in awe below.

CHAPTER ONE

Dr. Bernard (everyone called him "Bernie") White, 52 years of age and a prominent general practitioner at the giant University of Chicago Medical Clinic, sat at his desk examining the test results lying before him under the desk lamp's bright light. It was almost eight p.m., later than he usually stayed at the office, and the silence in the hallway was only occasionally disturbed by a passing custodian cleaning up after the day's activities. He had to remind himself that only a few floors below lay the pulsating, active hospital wards with several emergency cases arriving every hour to join the hundreds of predetermined residents.

He leaned back in the comfortably worn leather chair he had brought with him from his old private office, and glanced out the window overlooking the core of the city. Thousands of bright lights flickered through the falling snow and he wondered to himself what all those other people were doing on this cold winter night.

Deep in thought, he stood to stare into the infinite darkness outside as his mind automatically flashed back over his life, and prominently, on his late wife, Ellen.

He fondly remembered the many wonderful years they had spent together, sacrificing so much so that he could earn his medical degree. He recalled with sudden emotion the time he had found Ellen crying uncontrollably when she was finally convinced she could not bear children. He felt the familiar dull ache deep inside return as he thought of how brave and wonderful she had been all those years, while pretending it really didn't matter.

His thoughts then focused on the most agonizing day of his life. He had been at his private office, and pictured vividly how he was casually returning a patient's file to his secretary when she looked up, her face reflecting deep concern, and said,

"Excuse me, Doctor, but there's an urgent call on your private line."

He hadn't had time to theorize what could have such importance when he heard those first words:

"Bernie? Listen, I want you to please stay calm...".

Bernie immediately recognized the voice of his good friend and associate, Dr. Gerry Silver. He and Ellen had known Gerry and his wife, Charlotte (or 'Charley' as everyone called her), for several years.

"It's Ellen, Bernie......

Bernie remembered somewhat fuzzily the numbness that had overcome him as he had listened, unable to believe anything really serious had happened to his lovely wife.

Suddenly, he was there -- back in time -- reliving those few torturous hours all over again.

"Bernie? Are you there?" Gerry's voice boomed anxiously on the other end of the wire.

Bernie drew in a deep breath and answered loudly,

"Yes, I'm here, Gerry. Tell me what's wrong. Has something happened to Ellen? Where is she?" He was visibly trembling now and thankful that Gerry couldn't see him at this moment.

"Bernie, I want you to sit down first, okay?"

"Sure, Gerry..." he answered, his stance frozen in a standing position. "Now tell me what in the world is going on."

"El...Ellen..." Gerry began to-stammer unintentionally, obviously overwrought with emotion himself. "Ellen was in a car accident, Bernie ... five cars involved...on Highway 34... only one man survived... extremely inebriated... caused the accident...". Gerry's words began to fade as the depths of Bernie's subconscious succumbed to his conscious bidding for self-preservation.

"....felt no pain ... I can tell you that...".

Suddenly, Bernie's mind snapped and he slammed his fist painfully on his desk, his other hand tightly gripping the telephone.

"How, Gerry, HOW? You're telling me my wife ... my only reason for living, is dead and...'had no pain' Gerry? Just like that?"

Gerry recognized the first signs of hysteria and immediately lapsed into 'standard procedure' out of pure indoctrination. He hastily scribbled a note instructing his nurse to call on Bernie's other line and tell his assistant what was happening. He forced himself to try not to think about the fact that this was his closest friend he was talking to.

"Listen, I know how you must feel ... well, I guess I can't truthfully say that..." he hesitated, realizing he was doing a terrible job of trying to keep Bernie calm, then continued, "but I'm sure that everything possible was done... it was just <u>no</u> use Bernie." By now it was too late -- Gerry had given in to his own innermost feelings. "As far as we can tell, she was killed at the moment of impact."

Gerry paused as he listened emotionally to Bernie's quiet sobs, then tried his best to speak in an even, reassuring tone of voice.

"Ellen was at our house visiting Charley just before it happened... I ... I just talked to Charley, Bernie...she said Ellen was in a really great mood -- happier than she'd seen her in months. And just before Ellen left, she told Charley she was going 'home' to wait for you..."

Gerry realized his words were beginning to spill over each other, and again took a moment to calm himself down before continuing.

Bernie, however, wasn't even listening anymore as Gerry went on to say how they would be willing to help any way they could. Bernie was thinking of Ellen's last words to Charley, and suddenly, a feeling of solitude crept over him -- a kind of loving warmth. "I'm probably in shock," he told himself unconvincingly. "...wait for him at 'home'," Ellen had said. The words seemed to hang in midair -- it seemed so strange that Ellen had used the word 'home' when she had always referred to their modest contemporary apartment as simply that -- "the apartment". He knew she had longed for a real house of their own that she could really call 'home ', and just last week they had decided to start looking for one ...

". . we who know and loved her should all be thankful for that," Gerry was saying kindly.

Gradually, Bernie realized he was having difficulty holding the phone as a dull, throbbing pain in his fingertips worsened and began spreading rapidly up his am. He tried desperately to fight back the waves of nauseousness that tumbled over him, and squinted, trying in vain to clear up the red haze that was blurring his vision. Then, finally, he knew he could fight no more, and found himself giving in to the black void that was rapidly enveloping him.

"Oh... Hello Electra... I'm not sure I know exactly what's going on..."

" Really? " Electra answered mischievously. "Your body just had a heart attack."

"I know that. I just want to know <u>why</u> it happened." Rosamond countered immediately, slightly annoyed with her frivolous attitude.

In the form of two pinpoints of light on an uppermost shelf of the bookcase, they were watching the goings on in the room below. Bernie's nurse was beginning cardiopulmonary resuscitation on the pale, sick-looking body now lying haphazardly on the floor. Electra waited purposefully until Rosamond skeptically noted his body responding favorably to his nurse's valiant efforts.

"See?" She said playfully. "Nothing to worry about."

Rosamond hesitated, then said, slightly mollified, "Well, I still want to know why it happened in the first place. I certainly have quite a bit to accomplish before my physical passing, and this handicap was not part of my plans...".

"You are quite correct," Electra interrupted, serious now. "However, the speakers felt this experience was necessary in order for you to successfully complete your requisite accomplishments."

Why?"

Bernie forced his heavy eyelids open slightly and tried to focus on the white-uniformed figure before him while realizing he was inside a moving ambulance.

"I can't tell you <u>'why'</u> you had this attack just yet, Dr. White," the figure was saying, "but please -- try to remain quiet just a while longer. We're almost at the hospital now." Seconds later the ambulance swerved into the emergency entrance of the nearest hospital, which happened to be the University of Chicago Medical Clinic.

At about this same moment of physical time, Electra slipped easily back into her subconscious dwelling, just in time to supervise an upcoming dream sequence during a short afternoon nap.

Bernie had later learned how his nurse was credited with saving his life. She had used those few precious moments while waiting for the ambulance to administer cardiopulmonary resuscitation, regaining a faint but steady heartbeat.

The squealing siren of a passing police car pulled Bernie back to the present for a moment. He sighed heavily, then let his thoughts drift back once more to that terrible time of his life.

He had been unable to go to Ellen's funeral because of his own incapacitation, and had lain in miserable solitude for weeks following his heart attack. He felt unable to face the real world outside his room without his loving wife at his side.

Then, gradually, with the generous tenderness and thoughtfulness of many friends, especially Gerry and Charley, Bernie's life began to take shape once again. No one ever mentioned how serious Bernie's condition was – after a battery of tests and an angiogram, the results showed he had congestive heart failure. He had undergone an angioplasty which helped stabilize him for a while, but he knew that without a miracle he had only one--or two if he was lucky--more years to live.

That was one reason he had given up his private practice to join Gerry at the clinic. He felt more secure in the knowledge that when his final days of life came, he would not be deserting all the patients that had counted on him alone before. At least at the clinic there were always many other doctors to take one's place immediately, if needed. And with his medication, he could carry on a fairly normal lifestyle, at least for a while.

Bernie's focus cleared as he shook his head slightly to rend his mind free of any other thoughts of the past, forcing himself to think of the present. He knew, of course, that he could never replace his sweet Ellen, but well-meaning friends had finally convinced him he needed some social contact or he would become stagnant -- something he couldn't even imagine happening. At least he had finally made an effort to attend a handful of the many parties and dinners he was invited to, and his friends now seemed less concerned about his well-being.

He thought of Jenny -- so bright, cheerful and witty. They had been introduced at one of Gerry and Charley's dinner parties and had been dating casually for the past two months. It had been a little over a year now since Ellen had suffered her fatal accident.

He had told Jenny he'd be over for dinner tonight, but wasn't sure now if he could keep up a happy facade after his sad recollections a moment ago. He pictured Jenny's smiling young face -- always so vibrant and alive -- and wondered if he should call her and cancel the date.

In the quiet moment that passed, Bernie, much to his surprise, felt his melancholy sadness slowly dissipate and float away -- as if carried by some inanimate force. He found himself resolving to live the rest of his short life accomplishing whatever beneficial things he could, and not linger in self-pity as he waited out the days he had left.

He strode purposefully out the door and down to the lobby, pushing through the revolving doors into the brisk, fresh air of that cold October night.

Jenny Perrino was a registered nurse at the clinic, and as a result, she and Bernie were able to sit and talk about the medical profession -- a subject many women would find dull and uninteresting. It seemed to Jenny that Bernie spent a great deal of their evenings together talking about their field but she supposed it was his way of relaxing and getting to know her. Charley had told Jenny all about his wife's accident so she could better understand this complex, but warm and likable man.

Jenny was Charley's age, all of 34. She was tall, and what Charley teasingly called "voluptuous", with long, dark brown hair and flawless olive-colored skin that boasted of her Italian descent. She had remained single over the years, even after several proposals of marriage, knowing she was looking for something special in an important relationship like she was taught marriage should be. Her previous suitors had always seemed lacking in one or more of her expectations. So, here she was, rapidly fading into spinsterhood, much to her parents' dismay.

Yet now, she found herself inexplicably attracted to Dr. Bernard White, a man many years her senior, and a man still obviously feeling the sorrowful effects of losing someone he had loved very, very, much. She hadn't tried to analyze her feelings about Bernie, as she had always done with others in the past. She just felt so "right" around him that she told herself even if things never worked out between them, she would be happy and very thankful for all of the wonderful moments they spent together.

Jenny loved to cook, but rarely did so since her profession limited her time so severely and, most of all, she didn't enjoy cooking only for herself. So, it was nights like this when she felt happy and warm all over, knowing that someone she really cared about was due to arrive shortly for dinner. She felt a delightful sense of accomplishment while preparing one of her favorite specialties -- Veal Alla "Perrino". It made her laugh aloud to even think of the name. She knew that her mother would faint if she found out that her famous veal scaloppini recipe had been altered -- even ever so slightly -- by her well-meaning daughter.

Happily humming a cheerful tune, she uncorked one of the flask bottles of Chianti she kept in seemingly ridiculous quantities around her household. She dipped her nose toward the spout and sniffed the delightfully familiar aroma of her favorite wine.

Meanwhile, Bernie, down in the lobby of Jenny's apartment building, stopped to study his reflection in the ceiling-to-floor mirrors adjacent to the elevators. Her ran his fingers haphazardly through the thick strands of graying hair which seemed to be constantly in disarray. Glancing over the rest of his appearance, he felt reassured that no telltale signs of his deteriorating health were evident.

He sighed heavily as he recalled how Gerry and Charley were always telling him how pleased they were that he was seeing Jenny. They always said the same words meant to compliment him: "You're one of those lucky guys who gets even handsomer as he matures," or something to that effect. Then Charley would always start giggling and Gerry would slap him on the back good naturedly, and they would let the subject drop -- at least until the next time they saw him.

His thoughts vanished as the elevator arrived, and he stepped in alone, feeling a sense of composure lapsing over him. That familiar warmth encircled him once again, like a soft and gentle caress to instill strength and serenity in one's ailing physical body.

Feeling somehow slightly rejuvenated, he exited the elevator on the 15th floor, walked to apartment number 1502, and pressed the buzzer. Within seconds, a vivacious and smiling Jenny greeted him with what always seemed to Bernie to be an overwhelming amount of warmth and openness. "Hi," she said, smiling up into his ruggedly handsome face.

"Hi yourself," He answered happily as he embraced her lightly and closed the door simultaneously. "Mmm..., what smells so good? Not another of your Italian 'specialties' I hope -- I've gained five pounds in the last month alone from your good cooking."

She laughed and took his hand, countering playfully, "Yes, it just happens to be another Italian dish -- but this one is my <u>very</u> favorite." She winked at him and added, "I always save my best recipes for my 'special' friends -- I mean, I certainly don't fix my 'Veal Alla Perrino' for just anyone, you know."

They both chuckled at her dramatics as Bernie followed her toward the tiny kitchen where she was in the process of making a fresh vegetable salad.

"So, how is my favorite nurse this evening?" Bernie asked as he slipped onto a nearby barstool.

Jenny smiled and shrugged her shoulders seductively, "Well, you know how it is. Another tiring day at the office with the same old stereotyped patients -- the men all making passes or wisecracks; the women needing a sympathetic ear; and, of course, then there's the Italians ..." she smiled knowingly over her shoulder.

"Yes? Go on…" he prompted her teasingly.

"Well..." she began thoughtfully, "they rarely ever get sick -all that red wine and garlic, you know -- but when they do, watch out."

"That bad, eh?" he asked, feigning concern.

"No. That 'good'." She threw a carrot stick at him before he could answer and added, "How about a drink before dinner?"

"Sounds great. What'll it be, lady, a boilermaker or a stinger?" Jenny grimaced and Bernie smiled, offering, "Or perhaps you'd like to be <u>really</u> exotic--and try a martini?"

"How'd you guess I'd be so adventurous tonight? A martini is just what I had in mind." She ignored his snickering laugh as he went to the bar to mix their drinks, returning swiftly with the two glasses balanced easily in one hand. Jenny accepted hers and offered a toast as they raised their glasses in a salute.

"To our future health and happiness," she offered, genuinely.

Bernie's hand automatically directed his glass to gently touch the one Jenny held. while his mind tensed at the implication of her words. Jenny obviously detected nothing amiss, however, as she put down her drink and swung back around to her chopping board to begin anew slicing cucumbers.

Bernie sipped his drink in silence, chiding himself for automatically assuming her simple toast was anything but a friendly wish -- not necessarily inferring anything about their future together. After all, he reminded himself forcefully, Jenny was much too bright... and yes, much too young... to ever get seriously involved with a guy like him.

The evening passed smoothly and swiftly, as always, with Jenny being the delightful hostess and Bernie the attentive and courteous guest. He praised her on her expertise in preparing his favorite salad, and was visibly in ecstasy over her veal dish with its delicate flavorings and just the right touch of fresh basil.

"My Lord, if I keep eating like this, I'll start speaking fluent Italian," Bernie complained as he leaned back and rubbed his protruding stomach meaningfully.

Jenny laid her hand on his and said sincerely, "Well, at least there's one thing in your favor -- my mother has always prayed I would marry an Italian."

As soon as she'd said it, Jenny realized she may well have unwittingly stumbled onto forbidden ground. Her fears were mollified, however, when Bernie leaned over and kissed her lightly but tenderly on the lips, whispering softly, "If that's all it takes, I may just buy up all the pasta, veal, and espresso beans I can find."

For a moment that lingered into eternity, their eyes locked and all of the mental blocks and years between them seemed to fade away to some remote and faraway place, leaving them to realize, for just the few seconds that passed unhindered, that they both knew their futures were to be interlocked -- somehow, someway -- but they didn't dare dwell on it.

Abruptly, Bernie shook his head almost imperceptibly and moved his chair back from the table to stand. He picked up his half-full glass of Chianti and went over to her balcony window, where he became entranced while watching the snowflakes fall to the tiny nooks and crannies where they would gather and huddle together until the first rays of sunlight penetrated their hiding places and dissolved them into another form ... the water from which they originally came.

All at once an analogy began to form in his mind: the idea that life was known to exist as we know it for only a limited amount of time. Then, some believed, your body was given back to the earth, and your soul, as he preferred to call it, slipped away in non-material form -- some type of energy force, he presumed. But then that theory implied that your soul existed before you were born too -- and that posed so many unknown and inexplicable factors that it almost stymied the average mind to think if it.

"But you don't have just an <u>average</u> mind," a soft but definite voice from his subconscious seemed to remind him. "You've been blessed with the ability to research and probe and analyze -- you've witnessed and appreciated many of the miracles of the physical world around you."

Bernie almost felt as if an outside entity was influencing his mind, especially since he'd never even thought extensively in these terms before. Probably, he explained to himself rationally, it was just his preoccupation with his own impending death experience that was overpowering his thoughts this evening.

He had read a lot lately, as many others had, about the abundant theories being published on life after death. Now, he knew instinctively that he had to read whatever he could find in preparation for his own forthcoming physical passing.

He made a mental note to call Gerry soon to talk to him about it. After all, Gerry was rapidly gaining recognition as the most knowledgeable person in the medical profession on the theory of 'life after death'.

Suddenly, he laughed aloud as he grasped the irony of his best friend's expertise. As he turned to see Jenny staring at him questioningly, he immediately realized his solitary laughter must have appeared rather strange to her, to say the least. He forced his mind to temporarily repress all the deep thoughts he was so intent upon, and smiled reassuringly at her, satisfied to see her relax and return-the smile.

"Let me in on the joke?" Jenny asked as she joined Bernie at the window. She loved her apartment, so high above the city...especially on evenings like this -- frosty and clear -- when a white blanket of snow enveloped all of the brown and sooty buildings and transformed them into white, sparkling palaces, shimmering in the quiet moonlight.

Bernie followed her gaze to the delicate snowfall outside and answered, "Would you believe I was watching the snowflakes and thinking about where they came from?" He paused, then added, "And ... where they're going?"

Jenny looked up into his eyes, suddenly serious. Bernie slipped his am around her shoulders and continued. "I began to think of our lives and deaths, and what happens to us ... well ... after..."

They were both silent for a moment and then Jenny smiled and pointed an accusatory finger at him.

"Sounds to me like you've been talking to our good friend and local matchmaker, Dr. Gerry Silver."

He grinned mischievously and answered, "Well, I admit that I have read his articles on the subject... tell me, do you find any credence in what Gerry has researched?"

Jenny hesitated thoughtfully, then said, "Truthfully, since you ask, I do find his material quite fascinating, and, well, I guess I really do <u>want</u> to believe in life after death." She paused, then added, smiling once again, "After all, you know what they say, 'it can't be much worse than our life here on Earth' -- actually, I'm convinced it will be quite nice…"

"I'm with you," he agreed casually. "I just find it a very reassuring way of handling the idea of one's eventual death.--.but, listen -- let's not dwell on it. I don't know how we got on the subject to begin with."

They returned to the couch with their wine and the conversation drifted easily back into the safer territory of the latest articles in the JAMA magazine.

Finally, the flask of Chianti empty, Bernie stood and stretched slightly. "It's getting late, m'lady, and we can't have your glass slippers changing into... ah...moccasins, now can we?" he teased.

"Moccasins?" Jenny echoed hysterically.

"Okay, so I never was much on fairy tales," he admitted playfully.

Jenny walked him to the door and handed him his overcoat, leaning close to him. She savored the momentary feeling of security as she wrapped her arms around his broad shoulders and felt his reciprocal embrace.

"Will the doctor pay another visit soon?" she asked in a sultry voice.

"The 'doctor' had better watch out," he began, as he pulled her soft, warm body even closer to his, "or I may never leave to begin with. And then what would your mama and papa say?"

She laughed seductively and answered truthfully "I'm afraid mama and papa gave up hope of me leading a moral life a long time ago. If it wasn't for my 'respectable profession' as a registered nurse, they probably wouldn't even speak to me."

"Such a disgrace to your heritage..." Bernie said softly as he traced the curves of her sensuous mouth with his fingertip.

"Oh, Bernie," Jenny gasped as she melted her willing body into his. They kissed passionately and lingered moments after, with their hearts pounding wildly within each other's closeness. Slowly, Bernie pulled away and gently tilted her tiny chin up so their eyes met once again.

"I really better leave, Jen ... we both have to get up early in the morning." Even as he was saying the words, he silently chastised himself for not being able to handle the situation. Why was he always so confused at moments like this?

Jenny nodded reluctantly and opened the door, watching him walk down the hall to the elevator.

"I miss him already and he's not even out of my sight." she thought ruefully. Then, as she turned and re-entered her apartment, she told herself determinedly, "I'm gonna marry that man."

Later, after rinsing the dishes and putting them in the dishwasher, Jenny turned off the lights and music and went to dress for bed. She realized, as she changed into her nightgown, just how tired she felt and was grateful to sink down into her soft feather mattress. At first, her mind raced over the day's event and she made mental reminders for tomorrow. Then, slowly, and without purpose, she slipped into a quietly peaceful slumber.

"Matters are progressing well, Electra."

"Yes...I was pleased that we were able to perceive a mental glimpse tonight of the interrelated 'futures' in our current physical states."

"Soon your soulmate will be seeking your advice and knowledge in this realm when he finds himself here after his physical termination"

The private humor of the situation passed unheard between them, as did their thoughts, which needed no time-consuming verbalization.

Sensing a slight twinge of uncertainty on Electra's part, the Speakers added assuringly, "We will be monitoring the entire transition, Electra.   This is a most important step in the education of the physical entities in the present reality you occupy."

"Thank you. I am sure we will be extremely successful."

Jenny turned over in her sleep, unaware of her subconscious wanderings, and pulled the blankets up snugly under her chin.

Marian Kirby, a plain, simple woman in her late forties, laid down the iron with a sigh and sat down at the kitchen table, reaching for a cigarette. She frowned as she recalled the promise she had made in church last Sunday to cut down on her smoking.

"I remember not so long ago when I hadn't even ever tasted a cigarette," she thought to herself sadly.

Her thoughts drifted back to that rainy day ten years before when she and her husband Harry and stood hand in hand saying their final goodbyes to their son, Danny. She always found it hard to clearly remember that day, and almost impossible yet to believe it really happened.

She remembered the happy day Danny was born. It was like a whole new world starting for them. Harry was so young and vibrant, and so proud of his new son -- he even brought that silly football to the maternity ward of the hospital. She smiled contentedly and paused to flick the ashes from her cigarette, savoring her memory of all the joy and laughter

Danny had brought into their lives. How proud she had been the day Danny's teacher talked to her about putting Danny in an accelerated class for gifted children, especially since neither she nor Harry had ever even graduated from high school.

Danny had loved sports, and it was a rare weekend when he and his father weren't out on the street playing catch or over at the football stadium getting their fill of hot dogs with mustard while watching the local teams compete against each other.

"If only I hadn't let Harry convince me to allow Danny to go to camp that summer," she whispered aloud, rubbing her forehead hard as if to try to erase the memory.

She shuddered as she remembered opening the door and looking at the solemn faces of Father Riley and the man standing with him, whom she later found out was the camp director. Several of the boys had been down at the lake swimming, but no one had realized how shallow the lake was where Danny had decided to dive into the water from the ledge above, breaking his neck and ending his young life abruptly.

Suddenly, she was jolted back to the present by the phone ringing in the living room.

"Hello?"

"Hello, uh...Mrs. Harry Kirby? Chicago?" The voice on the other end crackled efficiently.

"Yes ... who's calling?"

"Brandon's Department Store, Mrs. Kirby. We thought perhaps we should check to see if you had inadvertently forgotten to mail your payment this month..."

Marian stopped listening without realizing it. She had grown quite accustomed to these regular calls from creditors.

"...due two weeks ago..." the voice was saying.

"I'll have to check with my husband when he gets home from work. He's probably already taken care of it," she lied, then added, "in any case, I'll double check."

"Thank you, Mrs. Kirby. I would hate to have to bother you again," the voice said coolly.

Without saying goodbye, Marian put the phone down and slowly walked back into the kitchen to start dinner.

At 54, Harry Kirby was slightly balding with a weather-beaten, lined face, and a well-earned beer belly. He sat slumped down in the front seat of his cab, relaxing. How nice it was to have a minute to rest, especially on his new route which included the Clinic. Suddenly he heard the cab door open, and laughed at his own wishful thinking.

"Three-oh-two Michigan Avenue, please."

Harry turned to look at the elderly silver-haired woman in an overflowing mink coat gingerly stepping into his cab.

"Yes, ma'am," Harry said as he started up the motor and drove slowly out into the heavy afternoon traffic.

"I just don't know how some of these doctors get their licenses anymore," the haughty voice from the back seat began.

"Jesus Christ, here it comes." Harry swore silently under his breath.

"Why, in my day, a doctor would come right to your home when you were ill. And they really knew their business too. You certainly didn't hear of any malpractice lawsuits back *then*."

Harry groaned softly as she continued to complain.

"It's simply outrageous what they charge you these days just to take your temperature. If it wasn't for all my poor, late husband's hard-earned money, I don't know how I'd stay alive."

"I'd like to solve all her problems for her," Harry thought to himself testily. "She damn well better quit blabbing about all her bucks or somebody will bump her off."

He was glad he was making good time on this trip, and soon pulled up in front of an overbearing Victorian home.

"Here we are, ma'am," he said politely as he reached back to open the door.

"Thank you, young man. You can keep the change." She handed him a $5.00 bill, and Harry shook his head as he glanced at the total on the meter: $4.85.

"Thanks loads, lady." he yelled after her, and cursed when he saw that she hadn't heard him -- she was probably hard of hearing too, he thought, damn his luck.

"At least it's quittin' time," he grumbled to himself consolingly.

It took him 45 minutes to get home through all the late afternoon traffic. Marian had just finished setting the dinner table when Harry opened the front door.

"Christ, what a day," Harry grunted as he took off his hat and overcoat. "Dinner ready Marian?"

"In a few minutes, dear," Marian called from the kitchen.

"Oh, damn it all Marian, why the hell can't you ever seem to get dinner on the table by the time I get home? Is that really asking so much?" he yelled as he stormed into the kitchen, waving his arms wildly.

Marian smiled bravely while reminding herself again that her poor, hardworking husband had to take out his frustrations on someone.

"Now calm down, Harry, and I'll get you a nice cold beer."

Harry grumbled as he popped the top off the beer and headed for his favorite chair in front of the television set.

"I beat my brains out all day long, listening to the half-assed problems of practically every Joe who takes the cab, and can't even come home to have a hot meal ready after a rotten day," he growled as he flipped the evening's paper open to the sports section.

A few minutes later, Marian had the roast chicken and steaming hot rice on the table, and walked quietly over to Harry. "Dinner's ready, dear. Come eat before it gets cold."

"That's right, damn it. Just as soon as I get comfortable, you come along and interrupt me. You never learn, do you?"

She patiently ignored his belligerence and went to sit down at the table, folding her hands for the prayer she so religiously practiced before all meals. Harry never participated, but Marian prayed for God's forgiveness and understanding for Harry's sake. He was well into a second chicken leg by the time she raised her head and whispered "Amen".

Their meal was finished, as usual, without conversation since Marian knew Harry hated to be interrupted while he ate. Harry pushed his chair back from the table, belched loudly, and walked over to turn on the television. Marian shook her head wearily as she cleared the table, then took out the vacuum cleaner and began to clean up the rice Harry had accidentally spilled on the carpet.

"Turn that stupid thing off, God dammit. I can't even hear the damn TV with all that racket." Harry yelled over his shoulder.

Marian felt her head begin to pound. "Sorry, dear. I should have thought to use the carpet sweeper so I wouldn't make any noise." She turned and quietly put the vacuum away, returning with the carpet sweeper in hand.

Soon the house was straightened to her satisfaction and she sat down with her knitting across from Harry, who was watching the evening news.

On the screen, a handsome clean-cut young man smiled as he read from his notes. "Here in Chicago today, Dr. Gerald Silver continues to conduct experiments at the University of Chicago Medical Clinic on several terminally ill patients, hoping to gain further evidence on his theory of proving life after death..."

"What a bunch of bullshit," Harry complained as he popped open a fresh beer. "Some crazy quack wastes all that money on a cockamamie idea like that. Now I've heard everything."

Marian smiled suddenly, pondering out loud, "Wouldn't it be nice, though, if there <u>were</u> something wonderful after this life?"

"Don't tell me you're <u>that</u> stupid." Harry burst out. "Now quit thinking about such damn nonsense and switch the TV to channel four -- the fights are gonna start."

Later that evening as Marian prepared for bed, she was troubled by recurring thoughts about the newscaster's statements about life after death. Somehow the possibility seemed very attractive to her, almost as if she had suddenly discovered a new reason for living...

The more her thoughts ran away with her, the more she repressed them, thinking it might be religiously improper to truly believe in such possibilities. So, she finally forced herself to lie quietly in bed and repeat the Lord's Prayer fervently until she lapsed into a fitful slumber.

She found herself walking slowly down the center aisle of a beautifully decorated cathedral, approaching what seemed to be a brilliantly warm light. It seemed as if she were floating, and the sensation of surrounding love was so strong, she felt tears coming to her eyes.

As she became enveloped in the protective embrace of the majestic white light, a new level of human understanding was reached within her inner mind. Such profoundness abounded that no conscious thought or word could ever express, and she accepted it readily – greedily.

Reluctantly departing the circumference of this holy presence, she gradually rejoined her more active and normal realm of dreaming; her conscious mind to be totally unaware of her lessons this night.

Gerry turned the car radio off as he sat in bumper-to-bumper traffic on the snow-ridden freeway out of Chicago to the suburb of Highland Park, where he lived with his beautiful wife, Charley, and their four children.

As he sat listening to the beat of the windshield wipers and watching the snowflakes floating down, he thought of the progress being made in his research. Only a few years ago, he would have scoffed at the possibility of proving life exists in some form after death. But now, with all of the new medical devices and advanced experimentation, he felt sure there would soon be a breakthrough in medical science as we now know and practice it -- a breakthrough that would change the lives of each and every human being on earth.

A slight shiver ran down his spine at the thought. meanwhile, his car inched forward on the crowded freeway.

His interest in life after death began at an international medical conference held in France in 1980. He happened to be seated next to a small group of physicians from various parts of the world who had been doing preliminary research with patients who were revived after being pronounced "clinically" dead. The more he talked with these doctors, the more he felt a sense of unexplainable excitement welling up within him.

Upon his return to Chicago, he began reading every piece of literature available on the subject, which only served to enhance his interest. He had been overwhelmed and pleased by all of the previous work others had done, even if not always for the purpose of proving life after death. Of special importance were the results of the test tube babies, -- in particular, those ovum that had been frozen after fertilization for over fifty days before implantation into the womb.

Gerry was currently very well known for making many important advances in the field, and had written several articles and a book on the subject. Most of his research was conducted at the University of Chicago Medical Clinic where he was always notified of unusual cases.

He had compiled several hundred files containing transcripts dictated by patients who came very close to death, or were actually pronounced clinically dead and then lived to tell of their experiences. Almost all of the cases described the same sort of sensation of leaving their physical bodies, floating up above in space, and watching the activity involving their unencumbered physical bodies.

Another common experience was that of confronting an extremely bright light. Many patients expressed the opinion that this "light" was either God or some kind of heavenly angel. The hundreds of other testimonials paralleled in several remarkable areas enforcing the possibility of life after death.

Gerry received several letters and phone calls each day as the news of his research prompted many who had had similar experiences to relay information they were previously afraid to divulge. Recently, many new books and movies on the subject were also bringing the public up-to-date.

Unfortunately, however, Gerry had no concrete evidence that would actually prove the theory. Still, he marveled at all the cases of patients being dead for even a short period of time, and who had come back to life with no damage to the brain or any other bodily function. Gerry's one hope was to correlate a method of 'monitoring' the death experience scientifically for, say, ten to twelve days or more, then being able to somehow re-animate the patient, classify his experience after death, and thereby finally prove beyond a doubt the existence of life after death.

It was nearly 7:30 p.m. when he finally reached his turnoff. He relaxed slightly as he drove down the tree-lined street toward his home, only a few more blocks away.

Walking out of the conference room, Richard Pearson smiled jubilantly after being appointed to design the new wing of the St. Peter's Hospital in Los Angeles. This appointment was especially important to him for three reasons: he was the youngest architect with one of the most distinguished firms in the country, DexterThornburgh, Inc.; he was up against stiff competition within the company; and last, but not least, he was black.

" It's about time they realized my real potential , " he thought wryly. The appointment made him the first black architect in the Los Angeles based firm to have this much responsibility.

As he strolled towards the door to his office, his petite blond secretary, Julie, looked up and exclaimed happily, "Congratulations. I just heard the good news from Sandy, Mr. Dexter's secretary."

He smiled and teased her lightly, "I see the infamous grapevine is at work again." They both laughed and after a moment he asked her, "Do me a favor and get Theresa on the phone for me, will you please? I hope I can catch her before she takes off for the airport -- she's flying to New York at noon."

Dick entered his small office overlooking busy Wilshire Boulevard seventeen stories below him. He was thinking about all of the opportunities that would arise out of this appointment, when he was interrupted by the buzzing of the intercom.

"I have Mrs. Pearson on the line."

"Thank you, Julie," he answered, putting his feet up on the corner of his desk. "Theresa? Hi, babe -- good news. I got the appointment. You know Tom Jenkins? One of the senior architects? He was so sure he had it in the bag, and then Mr. Dexter..."

"That's great, sweetheart," Theresa interrupted hurriedly on the other end of the line, "but I really have to run. I have a cab waiting to take me to the airport and I'll barely make it in time if I leave right now. I'll call you tonight from New York, okay?"

Dick dropped his feet back to the floor. "Sure... have a good trip." He hung up and turned slowly to look down at the tiny people moving about below on the street. After a few moments, he muttered, "Damn."

Suddenly, the intercom buzzed again, and when he answered, Julie asked, "Excuse me, is there anything else you want me to do before going to lunch?"

Dick hesitated only a moment before answering. "Yeah -- as a matter of fact -- how about celebrating my new appointment by having lunch with me today?"

"Why...I'd love to." Her voice sounded somewhat surprised but definitely pleased. "Just let me powder my nose and I'll be right with you."

As Dick cleared his desk before leaving for lunch, he thought wryly what a day this was going to be for conservative DexterThornburgh employees: first he gets the prestigious appointment, and then he is seen taking his pretty blond young secretary out to lunch. He was still chuckling to himself as he left his office and escorted Julie out of the building amidst all the expected curious stares and glances.

The "Fasten Your Seat Belt" sign had flashed off, and Theresa settled back comfortably into her seat. The first class section was not very crowded, so she had managed to get a spot by herself which she was thankful for since her day so far had been especially hectic. She crossed her long, shapely legs and shut her eyes while trying to relax. She was an exceptionally beautiful woman, thirty-two years old, with classic features, honey colored skin, and a great figure. Everyone always said what a beautiful couple she and Dick made. They were both tall, lean and very good-looking.

They had been married over nine years now. When they met, Theresa was already working for her present employer, I. Magnin & Co., in the capacity of saleswoman. Because of her hard work and diligence, she had been rapidly promoted to assistant buyer, and last year she became the head buyer for women's fashions. She loved her work, even if she had to do a lot of traveling, which left little time to spend with Dick. "After all," she told herself consolingly, "Dick has his career, and I have mine."

She remembered the years when she supported both of them while Dick finished his college education. There was always some friction between them during those difficult first years of marriage. Then, when Dick was hired at Dexter-Thornburgh, they rarely had much time to be together, and the tense atmosphere eased due to the sheer lack of exposure to each other.

"Would you care for some champagne, or a cocktail before lunch, ma'am?"

Theresa opened her eyes to see a tall, slim, blond stewardess smiling down at her. "Yes, I'll have a very dry martini, 'up', please." After a moment, the stewardess handed the drink to her with a tray of hors d'oeuvres asking politely, "Would you like some magazines to read?"

"Yes ... thank you" Theresa nodded absentmindedly, choosing a recent issue of the TIME magazine at random. She leaned back, opened the magazine, and glanced down the table of contents, noting with idle curiosity an article entitled "Further Research Leads to the Possibility of Life After Death" by Dr. Gerald Silver. She had always been fascinated by any kind of unexplained phenomena, so she casually flipped to the page indicated and began to read, sipping her martini slowly.

Soft music drifted across the bedroom from the clock-radio on the bedstand, and Anne turned over to glance sleepily at the time: 5:50 a.m. She stretched slowly and stared up at the ceiling, already thinking of the day's activities laying ahead of her.

Finally forcing herself to get out of her cozy warm bed, she padded into the kitchen to plug in the coffeepot. While the coffee was brewing, she buttered a piece of toast and spread on a generous amount of her favorite strawberry jam. "To hell with the calories today" she smiled to herself.

With a cup of coffee and toast in hand, she walked into the dining room, sat down, and opened one of the several large folders that lay on the table. "Needs more bright yellows and oranges" she said aloud while examining the layout before her. She made a mental note to talk with Sam, the head artist, when she got to the office.

She had been with McDonald and Smith Associates, a prominent San Francisco advertising firm, for over fifteen years, and now occupied the position of Assistant Vice President.

An hour and a half later, she arrived at the office. She liked to get there early and get organized before the constant deluge of interruptions began at 9:00.

Later at the office, she was about to pour her third cup of coffee for the morning when her office door swung open. Bill Anderson, her boss and Senior Vice President of the firm, walked slowly over to the opposite end of her large office and dropped down into an overstuffed couch with a groan.

"Is that any way to start the day?" Anne teased with a grin.

"Pour me some coffee, okay, Annie?" he asked wearily.

Anne considered the man sitting dejectedly before her. She and Bill had developed an underlying trust and friendship in each other over the years and she had been deeply affected when Bill's marriage had disintegrated to the point where he, himself, now seemed physically altered.

"It's your wife again, isn't it?" She turned and walked over to her portable coffee maker. "She's not getting any better, I assume." Anne knew how hard it was for Bill to cope with his wife's mental breakdown.

He shook his head solemnly, "She seems to get more detached from reality every day. I don't know what else to do, Anne ... I've had all the best doctors in to see her."

Anne handed him a cup of steaming hot coffee and said sympathetically, "I know Bill, but...well ... you just can't keep going on this way. You'll end up in the hospital yourself if you're not careful."

Without intention, Bill snapped back at her, "I just can't let her drift into oblivion. I have to keep trying to bring her out of it."

Walking over to the window to watch the trolley cars busily transporting passengers on the street below, he apologized, "I'm sorry for taking it out on you, Annie ... I shouldn't get so upset, I know... but I owe her that much... I mean, not to just give up completely..." He turned to face Anne directly. "You understand, don't you?"

Anne felt the knot in her stomach begin to loosen at hearing his soft, pleading words, and she started over to join him at the window when her phone rang.

"Yes?"

The voice on the other end delivered a quick message and she turned to Bill with a knowing look as she replaced the receiver. "Smith, Sr. wants to see you in his office right away."

Bill handed her his half-empty coffee cup and headed for the door, where he stopped suddenly and turned around. "Thanks for listening, Annie ... it really helps."

As the door closed behind him, Anne shut her eyes tightly, trying to clear her head of the emotional turmoil she always experienced when Bill appeared in this state.

Moments later she sighed heavily, then sat down at her desk and forced herself to quickly review her day's upcoming activities. She glanced over her notes from this morning at home, and rang for her secretary. Sally, a pleasantly plump redhead just twenty-one years old, promptly bounced into her office and chirped happily, "Good morning, Ms. Maybury. How are you today?"

Sally's freckles seemed to multiply every day, Anne thought amusingly. "Fine, thanks. Here's my schedule for today, and some dictation to transcribe."

Glancing at her watch, Anne realized she'd have to hurry to make it to her first meeting on time and gulped down the rest of her coffee. She picked up her notebook and told Sally, "I'll be in the third floor conference room -- should be about an hour."

"Okay, Ms. Maybury." Sally smiled efficiently.

It was late afternoon and Bill sat in a large leather chair staring hopefully at the man sitting opposite him behind the desk. Dr. Alvin Schottler, a psychiatrist for more than seventeen years, was concentrating on the folder which was open before him, his right hand lightly rubbing his forehead. Finally, he looked up at Bill, removed his glasses, and solemnly folded his hands on top of the folder.

"Mr. Anderson, you are aware of the great extent of psychiatric treatment your wife has undergone these past several months." He waited for an answer, and Bill nodded, thinking it was rather obvious.

"As you know, I called you here this afternoon to tell you the final result of these treatments." Dr. Schottler paused while putting his glasses back on, and then picked up one of the pages from within the folder.

"In our opinion, your wife should be committed to Pinecrest Rest Home as soon as possible, where she will be under constant supervision. This is not only the best place for Nancy, but I believe it is also a good idea for the preservation of your own mental stability as well, under the circumstances."

Bill remained silent after hearing his advice, so the doctor went on, confidently. "Please be assured that Nancy will receive the best in medical care. I will personally continue to see her once or twice a week."

Bill felt slightly numb as he sat listening to what he already knew was the inevitable. Nancy had become totally despondent, and recently rarely even recognized Bill. She seemed to float in and out of reality, sometimes speaking in a childlike voice.

"I've taken the liberty of making all the necessary preparations," the doctor was saying. "I also discussed the matter -- as best I could -- with Nancy the last time I felt she was closest to her normal state. I do need your signature on this admittance authorization, however, Mr. Anderson." He handed Bill the sheet of paper along with a pen, and pointed to the line where he was to sign.

Bill wrote his name, after glancing quickly over the information printed above it, then stood up and walked towards the door. Dr. Schottler went to accompany Bill through his outer office, where he added, "By the way, Mr. Anderson, I've arranged for a car from the rest home to pick up Nancy tomorrow morning around 9:00 a.m. That will give you plenty of time to go home and pack her things."

On the way home, Bill's thoughts drifted back to his early years of marriage. They had been joyously happy in the beginning, but then Bill started to spend most of his time on his job and it seemed that Nancy gradually lost interest in all the things she had enjoyed so much -- their beautiful home and all of her clubs and activities. She had always been truly devoted to many various charitable organizations. Now, Bill couldn't help blaming himself for her condition. After all, if he had only realized the effect that his spending so much time away from home was having on her, all this would never have happened, or so he had convinced himself.

As he drove up their street, his heart began to pound wildly as he saw the police cars and ambulance in the long, circular driveway leading to their house. He pulled up to the front door, ran up the stairs, and found

Mrs. Nelson, their live-in nurse, standing in the entry hall, wringing her hands as she nervously talked to the police.

"What's happened? Where's Nancy?" Bill demanded anxiously.

"Are you Mr. Anderson?" one of the policemen asked pointedly.

Bill forced himself to reply calmly. "Yes, what's going on?"

The policeman glanced toward the staircase and answered, "I'm afraid your wife took an overdose of sleeping pills, sir... they're bringing her downstairs now." He paused, then added, almost as an afterthought, "I'm sorry, sir, but she's been dead for approximately ten hours, as close as we can tell."

"I guess she took them after I checked in on her... as I always do, at 3:00 a.m." Mrs. Nelson stammered uncertainly, dabbing at the corners of her already reddened eyes. "When I brought her breakfast up at 8:00 this morning, I checked her pulse after I couldn't rouse her, and... then ... I..." she choked, and began to cry anew. One of the policemen helped her over to sit down on the couch.

Bill felt as if the world was spinning around him. He had left for work at 6:00 a.m. that morning, and hadn't wanted to go into Nancy's room for fear of disturbing her. Now he was hearing these words which seemed almost foreign to him. He could hear other voices echoing in his ears, but ceased listening to them. He found himself withdrawing into his own quiet, subconscious mind where the heavy weight of the terrible news he had just learned seemed to lessen somewhat. He was still very much aware of what had happened -- he knew Nancy had taken her life -- but it was almost impossible for him to accept it realistically at that moment. Instead, he let his mind lead him through the channels of memory that everyone experiences upon the death of someone close to them.

It wasn't until he recognized an annoying pain that he realized a policeman was shaking him determinedly with a firm grip on his shoulder, obviously annoyed that Bill was not aware of Nancy's body laying on the stretcher before him.

"We thought you might like to accompany her, Mr. Anderson," the officer stated flatly.

"Yes... yes...thank you..." Bill felt completely drained of all emotions and even thought fleetingly of taking his own empty useless life, as he moved towards the waiting van. He climbed in resignedly, lowering his head into his arms to cry.

CHAPTER TWO

Gerry walked through the revolving doors into the main lobby of the medical center and waved hello to the receptionist, who smiled in return. He took the stairs up to the fourth floor, one of the several ways in which he liked to keep himself in good physical shape.

The nurse on duty handed him two messages, one from Dr. Bernard White and the other from Dr. Ralph Hammond, the head surgeon at the clinic. He found out Dr. Hammond was in the midst of a three hour surgery, so Gerry headed for Bernie's office,

"Is Dr. White busy?" he asked Bernie's receptionist.

"No, Dr. Silver. He's expecting you ... go right in."

Bernie turned from the window as he heard the door open and smiled as Gerry approached with his hand extended.

"Bernie. How in the devil do you stay looking so young and handsome? If I didn't know better, I'd think you weren't a day over forty," he complimented his long-time friend as they shook hands firmly.

"Very flattering, pal ... but you don't look so terrible yourself, you know. It's too bad, too," Bernie teased, "I'd steal that wife of yours away in a minute if I had half a chance."

"You don't fool me, Bernie... I know you've got all those shapely young nurses chasing after you."

Bernie ignored the intended reference to Jenny as they both laughed and walked over to his credenza to pour two cups of strong black coffee.

"So what's new and exciting?" Gerry asked, as he sipped the hot liquid.

"Actually, I've been meaning to have a serious talk with you for some time now," Bernie began tentatively. Gerry's face sobered, and he lowered his cup, listening intently now.

"You see, I've been undergoing some tests here at the clinic to confirm ... well ... let's just say I'm not in as great a physical shape as I look."

"What are you driving at?" Gerry asked, already knowing the answer.

Suddenly Bernie's voice hardened. "Let's not fool ourselves, Gerry. We both know very well my chances of living out the next year are practically nil." He turned away from the bewildered expression on Gerry's face. "I am starting some new treatments on Monday..."

"You still have a chance then..."

"No." he answered firmly. "It's too late. The treatments may just give me a little extra time, that's all."

A heavy silence filled the room and neither man spoke until Bernie finally stood up and smiled. "Don't look so glum, Gerry. After all, you're the guy who insists things are so great after we check out of this place."

Gerry stared blankly out the window for a moment, then said soberly, "That's right, Bernie. I do believe in life after death. But that doesn't mean I can ignore my emotions when a close friend is going to die."

"Look, I've been thinking." Bernie tried to appeal to Gerry's professionalism. "Do you suppose I could be helpful to you in your research? I mean, as long as I've accepted the fact that I'm dying, and especially since I have a good idea of the timeframe involved, why not let me contribute in whatever way I can?"

"Listen pal, I think you're jumping the gun a little ... you should take a lot of time to make that kind of decision."

"I haven't got 'a lot of time,' remember? And please don't treat me as if it's my mind that's afflicted, 'Doctor'", he chided, forcing a smile. "I'm offering my services and I hope you'll use them -- if you think I can be of any assistance, that is."

After several moments Gerry responded hesitantly, "Okay, Bernie, I'll accept your offer. But give me a while to adjust to the idea, will you?"

Bernie smiled again, as he patted Gerry warmly on the back. "Anything you say, doc... by the way, are Jenny and I still invited to dinner at your place some night?"

"Why, yes -- of course. Charley has been after me to get you two over to the house for weeks. And the kids miss their Uncle Bernie, too," Gerry was obviously grateful for the change of subject.

"Great -- let's do that really soon, okay?" Bernie put his am around Gerry's shoulder, showing friendly emotion.

"Sure, sure -- that would be great," Gerry answered soberly. Bernie smiled and they left the office together in silence.

Bernie began the treatments the following Monday. The injections were very slow and painful and the entire procedure took the better part of a day to complete. Since the patients were not allowed to eat or drink during the treatment, Bernie found he was not only exhausted but famished as he left the hospital lobby. He had declined the nurse's offer of a hospital dinner before he left.

There were several cabs lined up outside, and he stepped into the first one, giving the driver his home address. He had recently gotten into the habit of taking cabs to and from the hospital to avoid all the traffic and parking problems.

Harry turned his head slightly to look at his passenger, and wondered to himself what such a healthy looking guy was doing at the hospital. "Probably just visiting somebody," he thought to himself as he pulled out into the traffic.

About a mile later, Harry offered, "Rotten weather we're having, eh?" He waited for a response and then glanced into his rear view mirror. Suddenly, he pulled the cab sharply to the curb and leaned over the front seat. "Hey, mister -- are you okay?"

Bernie was slumped over against the car door with his eyes closed, obviously unconscious. "Jesus Christ." Harry gasped as he quickly turned the cab around and sped back to the emergency ward at the hospital.

"Is he gonna be okay?" Harry asked the nurse after Bernie had been taken in for examination.

"Why, yes..." the nurse answered reassuringly. "He apparently fainted. He needs some nourishment and some rest, and he'll be fine. He'll be out in a minute."

When Bernie entered the waiting room, straightening his tie, he was both surprised and pleased to see the worried-looking cab driver waiting for him. "Sorry about the extra trip back to the hospital. I really want to thank you for waiting for me."

"Don't get the idea I did it out of the goodness of my heart," Harry laughed, slightly relieved. "You still owe me my fare."

They laughed and walked out the double glass doors toward the cab. My name's Bernie -- what's yours?"

"Harry -- why?" He always hesitatted before giving his name to people, even if they could get it off his license which was clipped to the visor in plain sight. He pessimisticly figured people only wanted to file a complaint against him or something.

"Listen, Harry -- how about letting me treat you to dinner tonight?" Bernie offered sincerely.

"Naw... I couldn't do that..." Harry was immediately ashamed of his earlier assumption.

"Well, at least let me buy you a beer -- we can go wherever you say."

Harry looked at his watch. "Well, I am off duty now, so... I guess ... yeah, okay." he smiled broadly. "I never did turn down a free beer."

Minutes later, they were at Harry's favorite hangout, gulping down the thirst-quenching ale and munching on the free nuts and pretzels.

Bernie started the conversation. "How long have you been a cab driver, Harry? I always thought I would like that kind of job -you must meet lots of different people."

"That's a laugh." Harry took another swig of his beer, wiping his mouth with his sleeve. "After you've been a cabbie for twenty years, everybody looks the same. And I'll tell ya' something else -most of 'em think I'm some kinda headshrinker the way they tell me all their problems."

They both laughed heartily and soon ordered two more beers. "Listen ... uh..." Harry began, trying in vain to remember his new friend's name.

"Bernie. "

"Yeah, Bernie ... they got a fairly decent chowder and steak sandwich combo in this joint, and since the nurse back there at the hospital said you could use some eats ... well, how 'bout it?"

"Sounds great. I haven't had a good bowl of clam chowder in years."

"I'll just go call the wife and tell her I'm eatin' out tonight." Harry stepped down from the barstool and headed for the phone.

By the time they finished eating, Harry realized he was really having a great time. He couldn't even remember the last time he had enjoyed someone else's company as much as tonight.

Bernie had told him all about his semi-retired profession as a doctor, briefly mentioning some 'routine tests' he was undergoing at the clinic. He also explained his habit of taking cabs to avoid the traffic.

They ended up sitting together and telling dirty jokes until nearly 11:00 p.m. Finally, Bernie leaned back and said, "I hate to spoil a great evening, but I'm afraid I better get home and hit the sack. I have to be back at the clinic by 9:00 a.m. tomorrow."

"Hey," Harry beamed. "How 'bout lettin' me pick ya' up around 8:30 and we'll tell some more jokes on the way there, okay?"

"It's a deal." Bernie agreed readily, felling strangely content with his new friendship.

Harry and Bernie hit if off so well that Harry insisted on driving Bernie to and from the hospital whenever he needed him to. One day as Harry dropped him off at home, Bernie teased lightly, "I really enjoy having a personal 'chauffeur,' only I'm afraid I'm getting spoiled. Are you sure you don't mind carting me around?"

"I told you I would," Harry smiled proudly, "but only if you promised to come to dinner at the house soon. The wife wants to meet you somethin' awful."

"Anytime you say, pal." Bernie said sincerely as they shook hands. "I'll see you tomorrow."

As he watched Bernie walk away, Harry realized how long it had been since he'd had a good friend. And Bernie was really a good friend -- he could hardly wait until Marion could meet him.

After he got home, Harry's thoughts about Bernie carried on through the evening, and he was exceptionally quiet, prompting Marion to be slightly concerned when be headed for the bedroom at eight o'clock.

"Harry? Is something wrong? Don't you feel well?" she asked worriedly.

He hesitated, then answered, "Wha? ... Oh, no ... I'm okay ... just tired, that's all. I'm gonna hit the sack early tonight so's I'll feel better tomorrow."

Marion accepted his reply, but knew it was strange for Harry to act like that -- he didn't even want to watch "Wide World of Sports" -- a program he never missed. But she knew better than to question him further, and decided to look in on him after doing the dinner dishes.

Harry had changed into his pajamas, and was sitting on the edge of the bed, about to turn the light off when he thought of Danny, his wonderful son -- his only 'reason for living', he used to think.

But now here he was, still 'living', still carrying on -- and maybe for the first time he had finally met someone he could really be friends with. Yet tonight he felt so overwhelmingly empty inside -- he couldn't figure it out.

Shrugging his shoulders, he sighed heavily and switched off the light, swinging his feet up on the bed to lie down. Almost as soon as he closed his eyes, he fell into a restless sleep, tossing and turning erratically.

He was back on the streets of Boston where he had grown up. Almost as if he had never left. He passed the drug store where he and his pals always hung out as teenagers and soon he found himself in front of the neighborhood theater.

It was always a special occasion for Harry when he got to go to the movies, even though all the films were quite old by the time they were shown there.

Today the movie was "Stagecoach" with John Wayne. Somehow, he was now seated inside, watching the great "Duke" do his thing. Suddenly, he noticed he was all alone except for the young man sitting beside him. Harry felt sure he knew him, but for some reason he couldn't identify him. He was very good looking -- could have been a movie star -- with dark, rugged features. Harry forced himself not to stare at him any longer.

As the movie ended, Harry and the gentleman next to him stood, and for a short moment they faced each other.

Abruptly, the other man smiled and hugged Harry tightly, then turned and walked up the aisle to the exit.

Harry stood motionless, rooted to the spot where they had embraced. Feeling terribly confused, he realized the emotions that bad passed between them had been extremely strong, and somehow familiarly welcome.

He was about to come to a conclusion about the man's mysterious identity when he felt someone's touch on his shoulder.

"Harry? Harry -- are you alright? You were talking in your sleep."

He opened one eye partially to see Marion kneeling worriedly beside him.

"I'm fine ... just having a dream, that's all..." he rubbed his forehead to clear his mind and wake up.

"But, Harry ... you were calling out Danny's name -- were you dreaming about him?"

Harry looked at her in surprise, then answered slowly, "No, Marion... I wasn't ... it must have been your imagination. Now let me get some rest, will ya?" he grumbled as he turned his back to her and shut his eyes again.

Marion straightened the blankets carefully and answered softly, "Yes, Harry ... you get some rest now..."

Most of the new fashions Theresa had ordered were already on display, with a few back orders still coming in each day. After checking the latest arrivals, she took the elevator up to the fourth floor, where only employees were allowed. It was nearing five o'clock so most of the office staff were cleaning off their desks, getting ready to leave.

She walked into her corner office, picked up the stack of papers from her 'IN' box, and sat down to review them. It seemed only a short time later when she looked at her watch again to check the time and discovered to her surprise it was after seven o'clock. She went to the office door and looked around at all the empty desks and offices, suddenly realizing she was completely alone.

As she turned and walked slowly back to her desk, she found herself thinking of Dick for the first time that day, wondering if he was home yet. She picked up the phone and quickly dialed their home number. It rang, unanswered, at least ten times before she quietly put the receiver back down. The stillness in the office now seemed to accentuate the emptiness she felt inside. She swung around abruptly, picked up her coat and purse, and dashed for the elevator.

On her way home, she relaxed a little as she pictured the evening ahead in her mind. She would take a short refreshing shower, put on her favorite negligee, light the fire in the fireplace, turn on some soft music, and wait for Dick to arrive home. She assumed he was out dining with clients right at that very moment, so she wouldn't bother fixing dinner at home.

By eight-thirty the scene was set, with Theresa curled up on the loveseat in front of the fire, a glass of vintage merlot in one hand.

The light from the crackling fire flickered against her soft brown skin and made her feel warm all over. She began to think of how it had been quite some time since she had felt so totally relaxed and deliciously sensuous. She sat up suddenly as she realized it had been two weeks since she and Dick had even made love together. It seemed that whenever she wasn't out of town, either Dick had to work late, or she was so tired by the time she got home, she barely made it to bed before falling sound asleep.

She leaned back, smiling to herself and thinking, "I'll make up for it all tonight. And from now on, I'm going to spend more time with Dick.

After all, we're certainly not struggling along, watching where every penny goes, like we used to. Now we can afford to relax a little." She poured herself another glass of wine, satisfied with her decision.

She awoke from a light sleep when she heard the key in the lock and looked at the clock, stunned to find it was almost midnight. The fire had dwindled down to a few smoldering ashes, and she had nearly finished the entire bottle of wine.

Dick looked slightly startled at first, then asked, "Theresa, what are you doing?"

"What does it look like I'm doing?" she stood up, swaying to one side slightly. "I'm getting smashed while waiting for my sweet, loving husband to get home from a night out on the town."

Dick took off his coat and hung it in the hall closet. "For your information, I was with some clients. We had dinner and then they insisted I go to their hotel for an after dinner drink. I didn't know you planned on getting home early tonight or I would have taken a raincheck on their invitation. You should have let me know." He walked into the bedroom and began undressing.

Theresa followed him in, the near empty bottle of wine dangling from her hand. "I'm so sorry. I didn't realize I had to make an appointment to see my own husband."

Dick turned around, took her by the shoulders and helped her over to sit on the edge of the bed.

"You know you don't mean that," he said as he finished removing his clothes. "I think you've had just a little too much to drink, and probably on an empty stomach, right?"

Theresa lay back, staring at his strong, lean, black body. As he was reaching for his robe, she jumped up from the bed and threw her arms around his neck, kissing his cheeks, lips and neck wildly. "Oh darling. I'm so sorry. Can you ever forgive me?" she pleaded huskily.

Dick dropped his robe and picked her up in his arms, carrying her over to the bed. He laid her down gently, reaching over to dim the lights, and then stretched out beside her and began slowly untying the silk ribbons on the front of her filmy gown, while returning her passionate kisses.

"I'm the one to be forgiven," he murmured softly.

As the negligee fell away from her shoulders, he moved his hands tenderly down her beautiful silky skin, feeling every muscle twinge as her body responded to his touch. He couldn't remember the last time he had enjoyed sex with his wife -- it had become merely an act of necessity to satisfy their basic desires, and rarely lasted more than a few minutes.

They were both in another world now -- no buildings to design; no fashion designers to argue with -- just an ecstasy beyond reality as they climaxed together again and again.

Hours later, their lust entirely spent, they lay quietly in each other's arms. Theresa nestled her head snugly under his chin, and they both drifted off into a restful sleep.

Theresa let her mind drift contentedly as she sank deeper and deeper into her subconscious dream state. Her diminishing consciousness was enveloped in a slow, floating sensation as the doors to this reality quietly swung shut.

Free now, her subconscious self sped rapidly across and through a myriad of universal dimensions, settling finally amongst a group of other entities, all quite familiar to her.

They were immediately surrounded by a cloud-like atmosphere as a residue of new knowledge rained down upon them, penetrating deeply to enrich and enlighten their individual 'beings'.

Then, the group merged together quite naturally, with her among them, joining once more with a universal energy force, illuminating infinity.

At last, spinning down, around, up and down, and finally through all the various dimensions and realms of existence, her subconscious crept back into it's temporary physical habitat, renewing the severed connection with it's companion, her conscious mind.

Theresa's mind approached the beta state abruptly as a siren blared loudly when an ambulance raced by outside. She sat up and rubbed her eyes, checking the clock on the bedstand: 4:00 a.m.

She groaned and lay back down, trying desperately to fall back to sleep. But something was strange about the dream she had been having when she woke up. It kept gnawing at the corners of her mind. What was it? Something about going to a kind of school ... she shook her head, puzzled at the meaning of her disconnected memories of the dream -- especially since most of the few dreams she ever recalled seemed always closely related to events in her every day life.

She stopped and turned to snuggle up close to Dick, dismissing her thoughts abruptly as she decided her rest was much more important than deciphering her dreams.

As the bright sunlight streamed through the bedroom windows the next morning, Dick turned over to give Theresa a good morning hug and kiss, but was stunned to find he was alone. Rubbing the sleepiness from his eyes, he found a note pinned to her pillow which read:

"Sorry love -- I had an early appointment this a.m. -- didn't want to disturb you. Call me later. Love, T."

Dick sighed disappointedly, then got up to dress. Within an hour, he left for the office, stopping at the coffeeshop in the lobby of his building on an impulse to buy two jelly doughnuts.

Julie smiled as Dick approached her desk, "Hi. Isn't this weather really beautiful?"

"Sure is," Dick agreed warmly. "Too bad we can't be outside to enjoy it. I always knew I should have been a mailman or something."

"Watch out -- you know what they say about mailmen and all those 'lonely' housewives on their routes -- I just bet you'd enjoy that."

"Come on, now -- be nice," he teased lightly, "or I won't give you this delicious jelly doughnut I bought for you." He waved it temptingly before her nose. They laughed easily and she followed him into his office with a fresh pot of coffee.

"So, what's on the agenda for today?" Dick asked as he sat down at his desk.

"Let's see..." Julie flipped open her notepad. "You have a 9:30 appointment with John Bartholomew in Accounting, a meeting with Dr. Bernard White from the Board of Directors of St. Peter's Hospital at 11:00, and, oh yes -- don't forget, Mr. Dexter wants an update on the current status of the Miller project by 3:00 this afternoon."

"Right, I better get organized here. You can help if you would bring me the latest Miller working drawings -- they should be ready by now -- I ordered several sets duplicated late yesterday."

His 9:30 appointment took only a few moments, which gave Dick the time he needed to prepare for his meeting with Dr. White. A few minutes before 11:00 Julie buzzed him on the intercom.

"Dr. White is here."

"Have him come in please, Julie."

Bernie's winning smile melted most of Dick's fears about this important man who could almost make or break his program.

"I'm afraid I'm a little new at this sort of thing, Dick" Bernie began. He smiled and accepted the cup of coffee Julie offered him before she returned to her desk, closing the door behind her. Leaning forward from his comfortable chair, he whispered, "Say, that's some secretary you have there -- can she type?" he winked knowingly.

Dick laughed and answered sincerely and a bit defensively, "She sure can. And she's smart too -- I'd be lost without her."

Bernie took another sip of coffee. "That good, eh? You better hang on to her pal, or I'll offer her a job with me in Chicago."

Dick realized that Bernie was just trying to break the ice, and he began to feel totally at ease, which was quite unusual for him lately. "You said something about being 'new' at this sort of thing, sir?"

"Bernie's the name, and that's right. You see, I only accepted this position on the Board of Directors last year to ... well...'help out a friend', more or less. It seems they wanted a representative from a prominent hospital on the Board, and the Director is an old medical school buddy of mine. So, well, here I am. Oh, don't get me wrong, I really don't mind, but I never dreamed they'd ask for my opinion in the design of a new wing. Why, I can't even draw a straight line." he laughed, then sobered suddenly, "Anyway, I'm going to be retiring from the Board soon..."

"Really? Why?" Dick asked, surprised.

"Well, you know how it is," Bernie hesitated momentarily, "I want to enjoy my 'mature' years." Mockingly, he stroked his chin, then queried, "Uh, what did you say your secretary's name was?"

"Julie." Dick smiled again at this friendly man he bad been so concerned about pleasing. "Would you like another cup of coffee?"

"No thanks -- I really better look over whatever it is that I'm supposed to approve and let you get back to work, or we never will have a new wing on that hospital. Besides, I've got to catch a flight to San Francisco shortly -- I usually make it a point to stop there whenever I'm on the West Coast."

Dick began going over all the latest working drawings with Bernie, who finally interrupted, "I'm sorry, Dick, but most of this stuff doesn't mean a thing to me. So, since the general floor plan layout looks fine, I think I'll just initial this for you now." He picked up a pen and scribbled his 'B.W.' in the lower corner.

Dick looked down at the initials and said sincerely "Thank you for your confidence, Dr. White."

"Call me 'Bernie', please." he reminded him as he walked over to the office door. "Now I'm going to see if Julie can take a coffee break."

Dick followed him out, a slight twinge of jealousy creeping up on him. He was relieved to see that Julie wasn't at her desk at the moment.

"She must be up in pubs ... I could have her paged..." Dick offered grudgingly.

Picking up on the apparent attachment, Bernie waved his hand and said, "No, no ... don't bother. I'll try again the next time I'm in town. Keep up the good work, now."

"Sure will. Have a safe trip to San Francisco Dr. -- I mean, Bernie."

The rest of the day flew by so fast it was 4:30 before he had a chance to call Theresa. Her secretary answered, "Oh hello Mr. Pearson ... Mrs. Pearson isn't here -- she had to fly to San Francisco unexpectedly. I was just getting ready to call and tell you that. She said she hopes to be back tomorrow, unless she runs into some complications."

"Thanks." He hung up the phone, then picked up his coat and walked out to Julie's desk. "I'm leaving a little early ... see you tomorrow." He walked off, leaving Julie slightly stunned by his strange behavior.

"Goodnight..." she whispered, knowing he hadn't heard her.

Dick walked into a crowded cocktail lounge, sat down at the bar, and ordered a double Tanguerey on the rocks. Four hours and too many drinks later, he asked the bartender to call him a cab.

Theresa paid scant attention to the maturely attractive man who chose to sit down beside her on the flight to San Francisco. Her mind was busily going over all the people she needed to see as a result of this trip.

"Excuse me, but have you any idea of the temperature in the bay area today?" Bernie asked conversationally. He was struck by the beauty of the black woman next to him, and couldn't resist getting to know her.

Theresa glanced at Bernie, as if deciding whether or not to respond, then answered, coolly, "Windy, sixty-five degrees."

Not being one to give up easily, Bernie pressed on. "Really? I thought it might be warmer -- it is so hot down in L.A. Actually, I'm from Chicago, and I can never complain about California weather. My name is Bernie White, Miss, uh..."

Theresa looked at his outstretched hand in amusement, then smiled as she decided she rather liked this fellow. She shook his hand and answered, "it's <u>Mrs.</u>, not Miss -- but I let certain perfect strangers call me 'Theresa'."

They both laughed, and proceeded to exchange descriptions of their jobs. Somehow, her husband's name never entered the conversation.

By the time they parted at the San Francisco Airport, they had traded business cards and vowed to keep in touch.

Anne let herself relax completely in the hot bubble bath. It had been a rough week, and she was determined to 'leave her work at the office' for the entire weekend. She closed her eyes as she let the warmth of the water sooth her tired, aching muscles.

She couldn't help thinking of Bill and the way he had been acting recently... as if he felt personally responsible for his wife's suicide. He had never come right out and admitted this to be what was bothering him, but Anne could easily guess. After the funeral, he never stopped by her office for a friendly chat as he used to -- only on business matters -- and even then he usually had his secretary convey a message to her. Everyone in the office had commented on his erratic behavior lately.

Anne wanted very much to help Bill during this unhappy period of his life, but could not seem to find the appropriate words to say and, more importantly, the opportunity to say them.

As the warmth of the water penetrated her physical barriers, she began to slip farther and farther into a totally relaxed state. Slowly, she closed her eyes and languorously stretched out her full length in the large tub.

It was a kind of spinning, drifting sensation – as if she was being guided by some unseen force. Suddenly she felt as if she had been purposely deposited at a particular point, which was followed by an extremely positive injection of warmth and happiness.

While wallowing in this unusual state of euphoria, she suddenly perceived a welcome communication – albeit nonverbal – which corresponded directly to the previously unanswered questions she had subsonsciously raised regarding the taking of one's life, in general:

A statement was presented for her understanding: To be an entity; a consciousness, a part of the current reality, one must abide by certain 'definitions' that are presented for acceptance prior to one's gaining admission to this particular reality. When any one of the definitions is purposely breached by a corresponding entity, the resultant actions on their part shall be unacceptable to the subsequent realm of being. Therefore, a separate set of definitions has been established to deal specifically with these infrequent cases and it is beyond the normal, average span of understanding on a conscious level to comprehend the sequence of events at this point.

Her relaxed state of mind greedily grasped the meaning of this brief subconscious interlude, then routinely filed it away in the depths of ther mind where her consciousness would not find it.

Realizing suddenly that the tub water was cooling, she brought herself to full wakefulness, and stepped out to pick up a thick terrycloth towel to dry herself with. Glancing toward a full-length mirror to study herself critically for the first time in quite a while, she turned first to the left, then to the right.

"Not bad for an old broad," she complimented herself out loud. "I suppose I really should have kept doing those chest exercises, though..." she frowned, as her profile showed a mere 33 inch bustline before exhaling. Actually, for a woman of 49 years of age, Anne had a remarkably well-kept physique. She had worked hard at keeping it that way, however, since she was not one **of** the fortunate few who could eat everything in sight and never gain a pound.

Her thoughts drifted to George. "George Wilmington Harrision, III." A smile automatically crossed her lips. She never could keep a straight face when she said his full name. It really was perfect for the profession he chose, however: Assistant Vice President at an international bank. Average height, conservatively cut hair, horn-rimmned glasses, with impeccable Wall Street suits, George had been introduced to Anne several years before at one of McDonald & Smith's Fourth of July parties at the Francis Drake Hotel.

George had been invited since his bank was one of the major financiers of her company. Being a very reserved personality, George could not find the nerve to ask for an introduction to Anne until after his third rum and coke, and even then he kept the conversation extremely formal. Anne could almost remember the words verbatim to this day:

"How do you do, Miss ... er ... Ms. Maybury..." George had said, shaking her hand vigorously.

"It's 'Mrs.', thank you, Mr. Harrison. Or may I be so presumptuous as to call you 'George'?" Anne had asked furtively.

"Why, of course,..er ... Mrs ... excuse me, is Mr. Maybury here with you?"

"Mr. Maybury and I have been divorced for twelve years now."

"Oh, please accept my deepest apologies ... I didn't mean to...".

"Please don't apologize, George." Anne had pleaded sincerely, then asked quite pointedly, "Now, am I to stand here suffering of extreme thirst, or will you volunteer to fetch me a drink?"

"Oh, of course. May I call you Anne? What would you like?"

"Yes, you may, and I would like a Vodka martini on the rocks, thank you."

Remembering how self-conscious poor George had felt that evening, Anne smiled, shaking her head as she realized how little he had changed over all the time that they had been dating. George was always the perfect gentleman, if not <u>too</u> perfect. He seemed to put Anne on a pedestal above all others, as if he actually worshipped her, and could not do enough for her. He was always sending her flowers or candy, and he even bought her a mink coat last Christmas. Anne felt very close to George, although she knew in her heart she would never accept a proposal of marriage form him -- if he felt prepared to make such a proposal, indeed.

George had been single all his life and still supported his mother, who lived in Merced along with his older sister, who seemed determined to end up a spinster at any cost. He once took Anne up to meet them -- which proved a most "forgettable" experience for Anne, to say the least.

George's mother obviously felt there was not a woman alive who could possibly be good enough for her "baby" -- so even when Anne presented herself in her usual highly attractive style, George's mother held her nose up, let out a slight "hrrrumph," and strode into the kitchen to finish supervising dinner preparations. George's sister was more amiable, albeit little, in that she at least carried on a facsimile of a conversation with Anne during the evening. Anne made a point to tell George that she chose to "pass" on any further family gatherings his mother or he might care to arrange.

Returning her concentration to the evening before her, Anne finished brushing her long brown hair and pinned it all atop her head, as she almost always wore it. George was due to arrive any minute and he was unfortunately always quite prompt on their dates. She slipped into a casual black wool dress, added a string of delicate pearls at the neckline and stepped into some comfortable black pumps to match. George had said he thought it would be nice if they took a walk around Gherradeli Square after a light dinner, so she wanted to be prepared for at least a five mile hike.

She had just finished mixing herself a short vodka martini with two large olives when the doorbell rang. She opened the door to see George standing there in his favorite pin-striped suit with a handful of yellow marguerites extended forebearingly, a smiling timid face hidden somewhere behind them.

"George. You really shouldn't have ... what beautiful flowers." She accepted them, feigning sincerity.

"I'm glad you like them, Anne." George beamed as he stepped inside and closed the door behind him. "Actually, I bought them two days ago at a corner sale and have been keeping them in the refrigerator ... I hope they last a few more days..."

"I'm sure they will." Anne laughed as she went into the kitchen to find a vase. "Would you care for a drink before we leave?"

"Well, perhaps if you have some rum and coca cola ... I guess it wouldn't hurt to have a small one."

Bernie's life had become a complicated routine each month: one week receiving treatments, two weeks working with Gerry and his staff, and the remaining time spent fulfilling his many other obligations.

It was late on a Friday afternoon and Bernie sat in Gerry's office, reviewing a recent statement made by a woman who was revived thirty minutes after being pronounced dead from a serious car accident. He had already read with great interest most of the other material Gerry had gathered in the past, and now he too was fascinated by the unproven theory of life after death.

Gerry and his 'team' of other volunteer doctors sharing his interest had compiled a complete medical file on Bernie over the last few months. They had agreed that Bernie should continue his normal activities, checking in periodically so the team could monitor the extent of his terminal heart disease. Bernie cooperated fully, and understood he would be confined to the hospital when it appeared that the disease was in its critical stages.

Being a doctor himself, Bernie had lived from day to day with the sick and the dying, and therefore felt he should be well prepared to face the prospect personally in a realistic manner. After studying Gerry's findings, Bernie was even more able to cope with the idea. If what Gerry believed and hoped to prove was true, only the human body expired, with the 'soul' or 'spirit' leaving the body to return to another realm. Almost all of the testimonies in Gerry's files related this sensation, with various encounters or experiences while in this out-of-body state. Then, they either willingly, or were compelled, to re-enter their bodies, at which point they regained consciousness in this world.

During the next few weeks, Bernie was scheduled to undergo extensive testing to prove that he was not extraordinarily psychic or in any other way significantly different from the average human being. Gerry explained this was necessary in the event they were successful with Bernie, in order to prevent others from suggesting some "abnormalities" to try to dispute their findings.

Bernie lay the file down on Gerry's desk and leaned back in his chair, contemplating what might lie in his future.

"Don't think so hard, Bernie. You're liable to damage some of those brain cells we've already so carefully analyzed." Gerry chided. They had both adjusted to the rather awkward situation they were in, and were usually able to work together in a fairly relaxed manner.

Bernie's famous smile spread wide over his face. "Okay, but just tell me one thing -- how do you expect my case to be the one to prove your theory? I mean, when I die, there's no coming back to tell you about it -- at least as far as I know about our medical technology." He looked up at Gerry's face and saw a secretive expression he had never noticed before. "Gerry, if there's something you're not telling me, I think it's only fair..."

"I guess it's okay to tell you now," Gerry interrupted. "We didn't want you to know before for fear that it might influence your behavior during our tests."

"Well? What is it?" Bernie could hardly wait to hear Gerry's idea.

"Come with me down to the lab and I'll tell you about it on the way." Gerry opened his office door for Bernie, who waited anxiously for the explanation.

"I'm sure you're aware of the theory behind cryogenic suspension..." Gerry began tentatively.

Bernie stopped in midstride. "You mean freezing the human body?"

"Yes -- with the intention of finding a cure, or whatever, at some future date..."

"And you're thinking of putting me in the deep freeze?" Bernie asked incredulously.

"Only until an appropriate heart transplant is located," Gerry assured him, as they again began walking toward the lab.

Bernie shook his head doubtfully. "I don't know about this idea of yours, pal. After all, you have no guarantee how long it will take to find a donor – not to mention the unlikelihood or locating a perfect match."

Gerry stopped before opening the door to the lab and nodded solemnly, "That's right, absolutely no guarantee. But listen, if you're not interested, it's okay. I'll be the first to understand...".

"Who said I wasn't interested?" Bernie said, smiling suddenly. "After all, you could say I've got nothing to lose, right?"

"Yes, but..."

"But, nothing" Bernie said flatly. "Now let's see what you've got hiding in this lab of yours."

After walking past all the familiar tables laden with test tubes and other miscellaneous paraphernalia, they entered another room in the rear of the lab. Dominating the center of the room was a large dome-like structure which Bernie immediately recognized as an updated version of the earlier cryogenic tube-shaped "storage tanks" he had read about.

There were various complicated pieces of computerized electrical equipment standing nearby, all completely unfamiliar to a bewildered Bernie.

"Quite impressive," he said lightly. "Does it work?"

Gerry laughed at his question and answered, "Always the joker, aren't you? Of course, it works."

"Good," Bernie nodded approvingly, the trace of a smile playing on his lips. "We eskimos like our temperature well-regulated, you know."

They both laughed, relieving the rather dreary atmosphere in the tiny cubicle.

"I just can't believe it can really work." Bernie chuckled. "Besides, I may not want to come back if the 'other side' is really so much nicer."

"I guess that's one thing we can't control, pal..." A look of slight apprehension on Gerry's face made Bernie break into laughter once again.

"Don't worry" he assured Gerry. "You know I couldn't resist being a part of such a dramatic medical breakthrough."

"I just hope you don't forget that." Gerry smiled. They walked out of the lab and into the hallway. "We'll see you in a week, right?"

"Right." Bernie shook Gerry's hand vigorously, his mind involuntarily dwelling on his upcoming unknown experiences.

Bernie spent the weekend with Jenny, as he always did lately when he wasn't busy at the clinic. They never spoke of his condition, but the strong feeling of a bond about to be broken was always lingering between them.

He had finally told her about his condition, since he felt sure she would eventually find out from Gerry's wife, Charley, and he preferred to tell her himself. Now that he was aware of Gerry's idea for cryogenic suspension however, he didn't know how or when to tell Jenny about it. After all, who knew if a donor would be found -or even so, if the subsequent transplant operation and resuscitation would be successful?

All these thoughts ran over and over through his mind as they sat on the patio enjoying a late lunch on a quiet, warm Sunday afternoon. The sunlight lay across Jenny's delicate face, highlighting her beautiful dark hair. Bernie found himself staring at her, studying her soft, perfect features. Suddenly, he reached for Jenny's hand and whispered softly "I love you, Jen..."

Jenny held back the tears she felt filling her eyes. "I love you too, Bernie. I always will."

Bernie drew her close to him, shutting his eyes tightly against the world outside them.

"Bernie." Harry yelled, as he spotted the doctor coming down the front steps of his house.

Bernie extended his hand towards the smiling cab driver. "I hope you've got some new jokes to tell me." he hesitated, then added quietly, "I could use some."

"Anything wrong, Doc? You seem kinda down..." Harry walked along side Bernie, a concerned look coming over his face.

"No ... not really...I'm just a little tired lately -- guess I'm not as young as I used to be." Bernie simulated a half-hearted chuckle. The truth was that he was finally feeling the effects of his disease, and seemed to be more exhausted each day.

"Well, listen, the wife's expecting you for dinner tonight. That ought to make you feel better. She makes the best chicken and dumplings you've ever tasted."

Bernie nodded and smiled, mentally making a note to cancel his date with Jenny that night. He began to feel better as they neared the clinic, after enjoying some of Harry's latest jokes, and suppressed his depression about his inescapable, unknown future.

Now, as Harry pulled up to the lobby of the hospital, Bernie said sincerely, "Thanks a lot for everything, Harry. You're really a good friend and, well, I feel a hundred times better after seeing you this morning."

Harry was obviously embarrassed at the compliment as he teased, "Just don't forget our dinner date tonight, or I'll be tellin' jokes about a cabbie who was thrown out on his ear by a half-crazy wife."

They laughed together and Bernie assured him, "Don't worry, I won't forget. See you at 6:30."

As usual lately, Bernie was visibly tired when Harry picked him up after the day's now strenuous activities.

"Com'on, Doc." Harry yelled goodnaturedlyas he swung open the cab door. "Marion's probably goin' nuts. We're already a half hour late."

The drive to Harry's modest apartment passed quickly with Harry carrying on mostly a one-sided conversation, much to Bernie's relief. Even so, he knew he somehow had to find the strength to be a worthwhile guest in his good friend's home.

As Harry drove down a plain, dark street, finally pulling up in front of an old grey walk-up, Bernie's thoughts sped back to his childhood when he had lived in a very similar neighborhood. A kind of wam appreciation for the simple surroundings swiftly replaced any concerns Bernie harbored as they walked up the three flights of stairs to Harry's apartment.

"Bernie, this here's the wife." Harry introduced a smiling, blushing Marion.

"Pleased to meet you, Doctor," Marion said timidly.

"Call me Bernie -- that is, of course, if I may call you Marion."

He bowed and kissed her hand gallantly.

"Oh, yes, certainly." Marion's cheeks turned a darker shade of red.

"Come on over here, Bernie." Harry beamed as he led Bernie by the arm over to the faded green couch. "Let's have a drink before we eat, okay?" Marion quickly exited into the kitchen. "What'll ya have? We got some bourbon, a little scotch ... and lots of beer."

"Whatever you're having is fine." Bernie sat down, then shifted to a slightly more comfortable part of the couch.

Harry poured two straight bourbons and handed one of the glasses to Bernie. "It's not much of a place, but, well, it's home."

Bernie glanced around the room and said sincerely,"It's very nice, and I noticed it's very centrally located -- close to shopping, schools, and..." He stopped suddenly when he saw Harry's smiling expression fade abruptly.

"Yeah..." Harry sat down beside Bernie, slowly. "We ... uh ... our son went to the school down the block before he ... died..." He stared down at his hands, fighting the emotions welling up inside him.

Bernie sensed the strong feelings Harry projected and refrained from continuing the conversation in that direction. In the silence that followed, Bernie remembered part of Gerry's theory -- the stories of a "reunion" with relatives, friends and others who had died previously. As he sat looking at the lonely, sad cab driver next to him, he felt an irreppressible urge to want to help him.

Their thoughts were suddenly interrupted when a cheerfully smiling Marion bustled into the room with their specially prepared dinner. "Come and eat." She called gaily, unaware of the sadness of the previous conversation or the topic of her beloved son, Danny.

Bernie took quick advantage of this opportunity to change the subject and leapt to his feet, exclaiming truthfully, "Oh. Everything sure looks and smells delicious, Marion. This is what I call real 'home-style' cooking."

Much to Marion's surprise and pleasure, Harry joined in the compliment by adding, "Yeah, she sure can cook, alright -- I can't complain about that."

The evening was a great success -- even Harry and Marion managed to enjoy each other's company, which Bernie sensed was a rare occurence.

It was only after Bernie was back home that evening that the thoughts of their lost child -- and the resultant loss of happiness in their marriage -- surfaced once again to nag at Bernies' weary consciousness.

Heading directly for bed, he tossed,and turned, trying desperately to achieve the hours of sleep his tired body needed so badly. Images of a small, happy boy interacting playfully with his loving parents kept flashing through his mind. The boy in his thoughts was, of course, the same as he imagined Harry and Marion's son, Danny, had looked. Earlier that evening Marion had proudly shown him a picture of Danny, taken shortly before his tragic death.

Spiraling slowly, effortlessly through infinite warmth and darkness, the surrounding void caressed him, yet encouraged his individuality until finally, like tiny particles of translucent dust they fell lightly towards their mutual nucleus. Gaining momentum now, the session was completed rapidly, with the various entities filing away their newly acquired information for future use. Unfortunately for their respective consciousnesses, these lessons were not always shared with their physical existences – but would nonetheless serve to enrich and elevate their true identities. Rosamond found, much to her pleasure, that Electra also had some fleeting seconds – a tremendously significant amount of "time" for them -- before she needed to re-enter her physical home. Even in different gestalts they were able to frequently coordinate these delightful rendeszvous.

"Isn't it wonderful?"

"What?" asked Rosamond, knowing full well what was going through Electra's 'mind'.

"You know. Soon we'll accomplish the most important part of our project. And look how smoothly it's going." She quickly sensed Rosamond's disapproval, then continued, somewhat less emphatic now. "Well, except for your unanticipated heart attack, I mean. But surely you understand that by now."

Rosamond hesitated purposefully before answering. "Yes I do understand. Much better than you, it's fairly obvious." Deliberately not giving her a chance for rebuttal, Rosamond went on abruptly. "You seem to be forgetting that when it happens, I won't be in this dimension. I'll be somewhere in between until we see if all the variables work out, in which case I'll return to hopefully complete the project successfully. But in the meantime, remember that I won't have use of my universal bank of knowledge as we do here. I'll have to depend solely on you, Electra, to help me 'cope' with my rather unorthodox situation when the time comes."

Electra had been listening carefully, letting the words really hit home this time, as she reminded herself of their difference in levels once again. Funny, she thought, that she should be expected to 'teach' Rosamond during the approaching transition, when in fact it was Rosamond who was far more qualified to be the instructor.

Electra knew that Rosamond had caught her quick thought about their upcoming reversal of roles, but was relieved when nothing further was said about it.

Their inseverable soulmate connection prompted her to answer simply "I can only promise to do my best, and, with the help of the Speakers who maintain the supreme direction in all that is, we will most definitely succeed.".

As they began to dissipate and speed swiftly to their destinations, another entity, by the name of Spiral, joined their excursion momentarily before they each split up into their individual awarenesses.

Bernie White woke up only long enough to pad over to close the nearby bedroom window before he stumbled sleepily back to bed.

Jenny Perrino remained in a beautifully peaceful slumber as she unknowingly hugged her pillow, wishing it was Bernie.

CHAPTER THREE

Christmas was always a favorite time of the year for Charlotte Silver. She had always been a highly creative person, and enjoyed making all the Christmas decorations out of something different and unusual each year. This year she was using various sizes of plastic bottles and containers -- the kind milk and distilled water came in. She had been saving them since the summer, and had accumulated enough now to decorate the entire house quite festively.

She gathered the children together and also invited some of their friends who had never heard of "making your own" decorations in this modern age of convenience. They sat down at the long table in the family room and began gluing various scraps of material, buttons, bric-a-brac, ribbons, and just about everything else they could find, onto the outside of the plastic forms Charley had prepared.

It was a happy, boisterous time for all the kids, and when Gerry walked in, it took almost ten minutes before anyone even noticed him.

"Hey dad." his kids chimed in simultaneously. "Look what we're making." Each child held up a partially completed project, dripping with glue and glitter.

"Hi, honey. You're home early." Charley gave him a kiss while holding her sticky hands out to her side.

"Glad you finally noticed me," he laughed. "I guess I should have come down the chimney in a red suit and black boots." he smiled, looking over at the tangle of happy children at the table.

Charley brushed a gluey finger across his nose and laughed, "Come in the kitchen and I'll fix some fresh coffee. How was your day?"

Gerry sat down at the table, wiping the glue from his nose with his handkerchief. "To tell you the truth, honey, sometimes I'm not sure I can go on with this research. I mean, there's so much opposition to what I'm doing..."

Charley turned around to face Gerry, and leaned back against the counter. "That's what I can't understand. Why do people want to fight against such a refreshing theory? Just because it involves death and dying?"

"I think it's been the same throughout history. No one wants to change -- especially a way of life that's been around so long."

"Even when it means a change for the better?"

"I guess so." Gerry stood up and put his arms around her. "Anyway, I've just got to go on and find the answer -- positive proof if there's life after death -- then people will have to listen."

"Ma! Hey, ma! Cindy's spilling food coloring all over the place." Bobby screamed from the other room.

"I better get in there before those kids decorate each other." Charley joked as she dashed into the family room.

It was the day before Christmas, and Marion was trying to find a present for Harry with the few dollars she had saved out of her grocery money. She finally decided on a light blue sweater, and was on her way home when she passed a Christmas tree lot.

She stopped, and her mind flashed back to the years when Danny was alive and Christmas was always celebrated with a nice big tree and stockings hung on the wall, since they didn't have a fireplace. She smiled as she remembered trying to explain to Danny how Santa Claus was going to get into their apartment without a chimney. She finally told him that she would leave the kitchen window ajar just a little so he could come in over the sink. Danny didn't think that was quite right, but Marion assured him that Santa wouldn't mind. Then she recalled how Harry seemed to change so drastically after Danny's death, and had told Marion not to waste any money on presents or a Christmas tree ever again. Checking her purse, she found she still had a little over $5.00 left from the money she had saved, and within moments found herself picking out a tiny little tree from the back of the lot.

When she got home, she turned on the radio to listen to some cheerful Christmas music while wrapping Harry's sweater. As a final touch, she tied some scraps of ribbon on the tree and then stood back to admire her work.

Just then Harry walked through the door, dusting the snowflakes off his shoulders. He stopped suddenly, staring at the small tree in the corner of the room.

Marion waited, prepared for the onslaught, but he didn't say a word. Instead, he turned around and hung up his overcoat, walked over to the radio, switched it off, and sat down on the couch, opening the evening newspaper.

After a few moments, Marion walked over a sat down beside him. "I bought it with the money I've been saving all year, Harry. I just thought maybe this year we could try to celebrate Christmas like we used to ... Harry?"

He slowly lowered the paper to his lap and looked over at her coldly. "I told you before not to spend any money on Christmas, and I haven't changed my mind."

Marion stood up, tears welling in her eyes, and said, "Well, I'm <u>not</u> sorry I bought it," and turned to walk swiftly into the kitchen.

Harry laid the paper down on the coffee table at his side and leaned back, his eyes fixed on the tiny Christmas tree.

He let himself relax slightly, and pictured in his mind the last happy Christmas he had had -- the year before Danny died.

Quickly, he shut his eyes tightly, trying not to think of it, but it was no use -- he could see Danny now -- running Into the living room so early on Christmas morning that the sun wasn't even up yet. His face was gleaming with happiness as he stood looking at all the brightly wrapped presents under the big tree they had decorated together the night before. Harry smiled as he recalled the biggest surprise of all that Christmas -- after all the presents were opened and Danny sat amongst heaps of toys and crumpled wrapping paper, Harry wheeled in the new red three-speed bicycle he had diligently saved for all year long. Danny had cried tears of joy and excitement when he saw the bicycle, and couldn't stop hugging and kissing his father.

A tear began to roll down Harry's cheek. He opened his eyes and brushed away the wetness with the cuff of his sleeve, then pulled out his handkerchief to blow his nose.

Danny had meant the whole world to Harry. He had wanted all the best for his son since he himself had been so poor and unhappy during his own childhood. They had so much in common, too. Harry had always been good at almost any kind of sport, and Danny seemed to follow directly in his father's footsteps.

Harry could hardly wait for the weekends to come so he could take Danny to a game. He even had arguments with Marion when Danny should have been doing his homework and instead she caught him watching baseball or some other sports activity on TV with Harry.

But then, all too suddenly, everything changed. His Danny was gone and there was nothing for him to look forward to anymore. No weekend football games, no playing catch in the streets, no wrestling on the floor ... nothing. His life seemed so empty now -- the same old routine day in and day out. Oh, sure, he could still watch the fights on TV, and once in a while he invited some of the guys over to play poker, but he knew nothing would ever take the place of his Danny -- his son.

Marion stepped into the living room and quietly told Harry that dinner was on the table. He stood and walked toward the kitchen, then turned and took one more look at the tree in the corner before slowly pushing open the swinging door.

The week before Christmas, there were always several cocktail parties and dinners every night to choose between for Richard and Theresa Pearson. All of the executives at Dexter-Thornburgh felt obligated to try to outdo each other, with the same thing happening at I. Magnin's.

There were dozens of boxes of See's candy floating around the offices, and the day before Christmas Eve, Julie walked into Dick's office offering still another box under his nose.

"You've got to be kidding." he laughed, backing away, with his hands holding his stomach. "I don't think I ever want to see another piece of candy after this Christmas season."

"I know what you mean." Julie agreed as she gingerly perched herself on the edge of the adjacent chair. "My diet is going to have an additional ten pounds to tackle come New Year's."

"Oh, come on now," he teased playfully. "You could use a few extra pounds on that flesh and bone body of yours."

"Listen. My men like me lean." Julie countered teasingly, striking a sexy pose and brushing her long blonde hair from her face seductively.

The room grew quiet and Julie straightened up, her gaze fixed on Dick's golden brown eyes. "Are ... will you be going to the Christmas Eve party tomorrow night?" she stammered unintentionally, her face flushing a light shade of pink.

"I plan to ... that is ... I haven't talked to Theresa about it yet." Dick forced his eyes down towards his desk.

"Oh ... I just thought that ... I mean, I'm not sure if I'm going either, actually." Julie stood up, picking up the box of candy. "I better go and finish typing the letter you dictated, or it won't get done until after the holidays." She laughed nervously as she walked out to her desk.

Theresa was in the bathroom taking a shower when Dick got home. After taking off his coat and tie, he walked over to the bar to fix a drink.

"Hi sweetheart." Theresa said as she came out of the bedroom in her bathrobe, drying her hair with a towel. "I'll join you in a drink. After all, 'tis the season to be jolly' as they say." She lifted herself lightly onto one of the barstools across from Dick.

"Comin' right up." He handed her a dry martini, with a plateful of stuffed green olives on the side. "Here's to a Merry Christmas." he toasted, lifting his glass to drink.

"Cheers." she sipped her martini, then licked her lips. "Ah ... that's good."

Dick walked out from behind the bar and sat down on the couch, propping his feet up on the coffee table with a sigh. "So, what's up for tonight? Anything in particular?"

Theresa swiveled around on her stool, laughing. "You must be kidding. We have invitations for four different parties tonight. Two from your company and two from mine. It all depends on what you're in the mood for: cocktails only; cocktails and Chinese hors d'ouevres; cocktails, hors d'ouerves and a light buffet; or cocktails, hors d'ouerves and a five course dinner."

Dick groaned at the mention of all that food. "I'm really not too hungry, are you?"

Theresa shook her head in agreement. "You know I only go to these functions to see what all the other women are wearing. It's always so funny to see all those 'high society' chicks trying to keep up with the latest fashions."

"Maybe we should take a night off and stay home -- just the two of us?" Dick suggested hopefully.

"Oh, honey, you know we can't do that. It's bad enough to have to turn down three out of the four invitations. I think we should go to the Baxters for cocktails and Chinese hors d'ouerves. It's bound to be the liveliest." Theresa put down her empty glass and walked over to look at herself in the mirror. "I think I'll wear my knee-length Givenchy, you know -- the red one?"

Dick watched as she posed for herself, making full turns in front of the mirror. "I think I'll go take a shower and get ready."

Theresa turned towards him, "Good idea ... oh ... by the way ...we're going to Magnin's Christmas Eve party tomorrow night at the Hilton, aren't we? It's a dinner/dance starting at 7:00 p.m. I need to reserve the seats to make sure we get placed with the other executives."

He noticed Theresa was back at the mirror, closely inspecting her face for any new wrinkles. "Yeah ... I guess so. My company is having a dinner/dance too at the Beverly Wilshire, but I haven't made any definite commitment yet." When she didn't answer, Dick turned and walked slowly into the bedroom to change.

On Christmas Eve, Theresa looked absolutely beautiful in her new gown, a Dior original she had ordered several months ago. Dick was also extremely handsome in his well-tailored black tuxedo, as they stepped into a cab to take them to the Hilton Hotel.

As Theresa had planned, they were seated at one of the most prestigious tables with several of the top executives of the company. After a formal toast to the holiday season, the crowd settled down to enjoy the evening of drinking, dining and dancing.

After forty-five minutes, Dick realized he had not spoken a word since they had arrived there. Of course, Theresa had been enjoying all the local gossip along with the others at the table, but Dick became increasingly perturbed at the entire situation.

"Theresa..." he placed his hand lightly on her shoulder.

"What is it, sweetheart?" she turned to him, beaming with false sincerity.

"I'm leaving."

Her smile faded rapidly and an icy glare replaced it. "Don't be ridiculous, Richard."

"You can stay here if you like, or join me at the Dexter-Thornburgh party, but I'm not staying here with all these sickening fakes." he replied with a tight smile as he stood up slowly. "Besides, I'm sure I won't even be missed."

"You're acting like an ass, and you know it." Theresa snapped in a low voice. "Sit back down and have another drink."

"Goodbye, 'dear'." Dick looked around the table at all the smiling faces, so engrossed in each other they didn't even notice their heated conversation, and then strode briskly out of the room.

On the way to the Beverly Wilshire, he began to have second thoughts about his leaving Theresa so abruptly, but then started to realize that he had always gone along with whatever she wanted to do. He sat back and relaxed, feeling a new sensation coming over him -- one of long-lost independence -- as he approached the hotel entrance.

When he walked into the main banquet room at the hotel, he noticed the majority of the people had already finished eating and were beginning to wander into the adjoining room where the orchestra was playing some light dancing music.

Smiling and waving at the familiar faces around him, he passed through the dining area and stood at the edge of the dance floor. Suddenly, his gaze rested on Julie's slim figure, wearing a floor length taffeta gown with a low-cut bodice, standing amongst a group of people in one corner of the room. She had her hair pinned up, with ringlets dangling attractively around her face. Dick found he couldn't take his eyes off her, and it was obvious that he wasn't the only man there who felt that way.

She turned and saw him standing in the doorway and waved, a bright smile lighting up her face. He met her halfway across the dance floor, and asked, "This seems like an appropriate place to ask a lady to dance. Would you do me the honor?"

She curtsied, then answered playfully, "Certainly, my lord ... or should I say 'my boss'?"

Dick made a face at the poor joke and they both laughed as he took her lightly into his arms for a brisk number being played at the moment.

They danced across the floor as if they had danced a thousand times together, floating in each other's light embrace. Finally, the orchestra stopped to take a break, and he led Julie over to the bar where they found two empty seats.

"Don't tell me ... let me guess ... a Black Russian on the rocks?" Dick asked breathlessly, still panting from the last dance.

"Well, actually I'd like a glass of iced tea, thank you. I hate to appear so naive, but I don't even know what a Black Russian is." She blushed suddenly as she realized what she had implied.

Dick correctly interpreted her embarrassment and assured her, "Don't worry, that's not where the name came from."

They both laughed until they had tears in their eyes and then stopped long enough to make a toast.

"To a very beautiful lady," Dick proposed, sobering slightly.

"And to a most wonderful man," Julie returned his steady gaze as she held her glass to her lips.

The rest of the evening flew by as they danced practically every dance and stopped only when the orchestra stopped, when they cheerfully refilled their glasses.

Finally, the people began to disperse, saying their goodnights and "Merry Christmases" to each group around the room. Dick sat beside Julie at the bar, both of them feeling quite relaxed after the evening of dancing. "Can I give you a ride home?" he asked, putting his hand gently on hers.

"That would be nice," she said softly,

Julie lived in a small but attractive one-bedroom apartment in Hollywood. As they walked up to her door, Dick stopped and let go of her hand suddenly.

"You'll come in for a nightcap, won't you?" Julie asked shyly.

"I really better be getting home myself, little lady," he tried a half-hearted smile. "It's pretty late to be out alone on these 'dangerous' streets, you know."

As if she hadn't even heard him, Julie stepped forward, put her arms around his neck, and closing her eyes she kissed him tenderly. Trembling slightly, she leaned back with a sigh, savoring the moment and hoping he would decide to say.

Dick held her for a moment, severely tempted to sweep her up into his arms and take her Inside. Finally, realizing he was too confused to make any type of commitments so soon, he looked into her soft blue eyes and whispered, "I'm sorry ... I have to go ... good night ... and thank you -- just for being you."

He turned to walk back out to the street, where he caught a passing cab.

For Anne, the Christmas season always seemed to fly by, with the flurry of high-cost advertising that most of the big companies were carrying out to promote their Christmas sales. No one ever realized how far in advance these ads were prepared. By mid-September, Christmas ads were well on their way to finalization while most in the company began to think in terms of New Year's and Valentine's Day sales pitches.

Anne made it a point to only attend a very few of the many functions given this time of year. For one thing, she found herself so tired after ten to twelve hours at the office, she barely made it home to the warmth of her comfortable big bed.

At least George didn't seem to mind, since he himself wasn't terribly fond of large gatherings. He seemed satisfied with their daily short telephone conversations, which were usually cut short by Anne's having to rush off to some meeting, or other unexpected interruption.

She had spent Christmas alone at home, since George had insisted he had to be with his relatives for a family dinner. Anne gladly refused his invitation to join them, and instead fixed herself a delicious steak dinner and spent the evening reading a good book.

Now it was Friday, December 28th, and Anne was rushing down the hall towards the conference room when she was nearly knocked over by someone who had emerged from a nearby office. After recovering her balance, she stammered, "Oh, excuse me." Looking up she realized it was Bill standing next to her and grasping her elbow firmly.

"Bill. I haven't run into you in ages." She began to laugh at her unintentional pun, then stopped when she saw that he wasn't smiling.

"It was entirely my fault for barging out the door without watching where I was going. I'm very sorry." His voice was cool and distant, and he turned and walked into the conference room, leaving Anne standing alone in the hallway.

"Well, I'll be damned." she said quietly to herself, and then joined the assemblage being seated at the long conference table.

Hamilton Smith, Sr. was seated at the head of the table, with the two Senior Vice Presidents, Bill and Smith, Jr., at each side of him. The Financial Vice President, the Legal Vice President, and Anne in her capacity as Assistant Vice President, took the remaining chairs, with a secretary at the far end of the table ready to take minutes of the meeting.

Finally, as Smith, Sr. stood up, an immediate hush fell over the room. He sat back down In his chair and cleared his voice authoritatively.

"First, allow me to thank you for interrupting your busy schedules during this holiday season to attend this unexpected meeting." He slowly moved his gaze in a clockwise direction, focusing momentarily on each person at the table, before continuing his speech.

"The reason I have asked you all here is to tell you ... I have decided to retire."

A low murmur of voices and surprised glances sped around the room. Raising his voice slightly to regain attention, he went on. "I'm sure that does not come as such a great shock to most of you." He smiled, lighting his pipe and puffing great billows of smoke into the air, while noticing a rising apprehension in the room. "The next question on your minds is who will be my replacement as President of our company." At this point everyone noticed Smith, Jr. smiling broadly, as he leaned back in his chair.

"The truth is ... I have not made a final decision yet." He noticed his son's smile fade abruptly.

Anne glanced at Bill, who seemed, if anything, disinterested in the important announcement being made. The President's statement meant that Bill was also being seriously considered. Anne shared the feeling of most of the other employees that Bill could handle the job much better than Smith, Jr., even considering Bill's change of personality since his wife's tragic death.

Smith, Sr. continued the meeting. "My decision will be finalized before the next board meeting. And now, let's get back to the real business at hand: advertising -- so we can make some money around here."

An hour later, the meeting was adjourned and Anne waited outside the room for Bill, who had been detained momentarily by the Financial Vice President. When Bill finally came out, he walked right by Anne, who had to rush to catch up to him.

"Bill." She took his arm and he turned to look at her. "I ... I wonder if you have a minute to talk." Then glancing around her, she added, "In my office -- it's closer than yours."

Bill looked down at his watch and said, "I'm really busy, Anne..." he hesitated, looking at Anne's disappointed face. "But I guess I can spare a few minutes."

They walked into her office and Anne waited for Bill to sit back comfortably on the couch before choosing a seat on an adjacent chair.

"I'm really not sure exactly what I want to say to you, Bill ... I only know I've been meaning to talk to you for months now, and I never seem to have a chance."

Finding it difficult to face him directly, she stood up and walked over to the window. When she turned back around after a moment, she found Bill's eyes staring directly into her. Just as she was about to speak, Bill said quietly, "I know what you want to tell me. Anne. Why do you think I've been avoiding you for so long? It's not easy to face up to reality, believe me."

Anne stood frozen still, feeling stunned by Bill's outburst after such a long silence. "Reality? I don't understand..."

"I've been going to a psychiatrist for the last several months now -- the same one Nancy was seeing. He even warned me I may risk having a heart attack if I don't stop blaming myself for her death. Also, I've been throwing myself into my work too seriously, he says, just so I won't have to cope with my feelings."

Anne walked over to sit by Bill, feeling a knot tightening deep inside her.

"I didn't know you were consulting a doctor all this time, Bill. I was worried you might be keeping it all to yourself." Without thinking, she put her hand comfortingly on his. "Oh, Bill, you must realize you aren't to blame. And besides, Nancy is better off not living a life without some link to the real world. You know that towards the end you said she didn't even recognize you." Anne suddenly realized she was raising her voice, and turned away to hide her embarrassment.

"I'm sorry," she apologized sincerely. "I have no right to talk that way about Nancy. It's just that ... well, I don't want you to end up the same way, that's all. And now, after Smith's announcement today, we would all hate to see you lose out on your chance for the Presidency."

Bill watched somberly as Anne walked to her desk, standing with her back towards him. Finally, he stood and walked up behind her, raising his hands to rest gently on her shoulders.

"Annie..." he whispered softly, meaningfully.

She turned slowly when she heard him call her "Annie" as he did so many times before the accident. His arms encircled her and she found herself overwhelmed in his light but warm embrace. A shiver ran down her spine as she returned his searching stare.

It seemed as if she had only closed her eyes momentarily when she felt his touch leave her arms. She saw that he was picking up the folders he had left on the couch as he headed for the office door. Just then, he turned and smiled broadly and asked, "Will I see you at the New Year's Eve party?"

"You mean you're _going?_" Anne exclaimed, regretting at once the tone of surprise in her voice.

He laughed and nodded, "I think it's time I attend some of the company get-togethers. After all, it appears I'm still in the running for President of this place, and a little 'politiking' never hurt. That _is_ what you really wanted to talk to me about, right?" He winked, and closed the door behind him before she could answer.

As Anne leaned back against her desk, she felt a wonderful feeling of contentment flowing over her for the first time in so very long. She wanted to rush out of her office, throw her arms around Bill and tell him just how she felt. It was at that moment that she realized she could never be truly happy until she had Bill by her side forever.

Later that afternoon, Bill arrived at the psychiatrist's office. He was smiling conspicuously as he sat down across from the doctor.

"My, my. You certainly appear to be in high spirits today," Dr. Schottler commented. "I'm glad to see you're snapping out of it."

"I've decided to start the New Year right." Bill answered as he leaned back casually.

"Good for you. Now tell me -- how have you been feeling physically?"

"Don't tell me you're still worried about my heart?" Bill asked incredulously.

"You admitted you were having chest pains, Bill. I only wish you'd have it checked out."

"I don't have the time." Bill snapped, slightly exasperated. "I shouldn't even be taking the time to come here. Besides ... I'm sure it was just acid indigestion -- or something else perfectly normal."

Dr. Schottler stood up and walked over behind his desk. "I'll make you a deal. You skip your next appointment with me and take the time today to go and see a friend of mine -- he's visiting from Chicago. His name is Dr. Bernie White and he's over at the UC Clinic this afternoon. I'll call him and tell him you're coming." He wrote down the name and address on a slip of paper and handed it to Bill.

"Okay ... I guess the afternoon's lost now anyway," Bill agreed grudgingly as he stood, extending his hand to the psychiatrist. "Thanks for putting up with me, doc ... and have a happy New Year, okay?" Bill smiled sincerely.

"I will, thanks. Just be sure you keep your word and do the same."

Bill drove the short distance to the clinic and handed the slip of paper to the receptionist as he entered the modest lobby.

"I believe he's expecting me," he told the young woman as she examined the note.

"Oh, yes. Dr. White is in room 613." She pointed to a hallway on the right. "Just go right down there and take the elevator to the sixth floor."

Bill found room 613, and opened the door to see Bernie sitting casually on the edge of a desk, intently studying an open folder he was holding in one hand.

"Excuse me ... I'm Bill Anderson. I believe Dr. Schottler called..."

Bernie looked up from the folder, smiled and walked over to greet Bill. "Oh, yes. What's that crazy headshrinker trying to do anyway?"

He laughed as he led Bill over to a pair of chairs by the desk. "Sounds like he's convinced your heart's about to give out. I told him he should limit his diagnoses to the mind and leave the rest to the MD's."

Bill relaxed as he thought to himself, "If all doctors were like this one, I wouldn't be so hesitate to go in for a checkup once in a while." Then he answered aloud, "Yeah, just because I made the mistake of complaining about some simple chest pains during one of my visits, he put me right into the heart attack category."

"Actually, I'm sure Al means well -- I've known him for years and he's always very considerate about his patients' well-being. So, we better take a look and put his mind -- and yours -- at ease."

After a short examination, Bernie removed his stethoscope and sat down behind the desk. Bill was buttoning up his shirt and asked, "So what's the verdict, doctor? The ol' ticker sounds loud and clear, right?"

"How old did you say you were again, Bill?"

Bill stopped suddenly, carefully studying Bernie's face before answering. "Fifty-three, why?"

"Well, it appears our mutual friend may have some basis for concern after all. Your blood pressure is extremely high, most likely because of job-related tension. Not 'nervous tension'," he pointed out clearly, "but 'hypertension'. I won't try to kid you, Bill. This could lead to a stroke -- or even kidney disease."

Bill sat very still, trying to absorb the implication of the words being spoken to him.

Bernie continued, noting the apparent state of concern overtaking Bill. "Now just relax, Bill. I certainly didn't mean to scare you, although I believe it's almost always best to tell the patient the truth about his condition." Bernie stopped momentarily as he thought of his own heart disease. Then, dismissing his own problems, he continued reassuringly. "At any rate, you seem to be in fairly good physical shape otherwise, which means you have many avenues open to you to improve or at least stabilize your condition."

At that, Bill began to loosen up a little, and leaned forward to say, "I'm sorry for appearing so shaken, Dr. White. I never realized I was really jeopardizing my health -- and especially now he thought of Anne and the warm, electric feeling he had experienced when he had held her in his arms so briefly. "Especially now," he repeated. "Please tell me how I can help myself."

Bernie's smile seemed to alleviate some of the tension in the room. "It shouldn't be all that difficult, actually, since Al tells me you seem to be overcoming your feelings of guilt over your wife's death."

Bill's eyes lifted abruptly to meet Bernie's. "Oh, he told you about ... my wife..."

"Yes, he did. You see, such traumatic experiences often relate heavily to a doctor's diagnosis and advice. But to get back to the subject of your health, you need to stop pushing yourself to extremes on your job. I don't know exactly what you do, but it's obvious you're under tremendous pressure. Perhaps you even create some of that pressure within yourself."

"Second, start getting some limited exercise regularly -preferably out in the fresh air. Cut down on the salt in your diet, and, if possible, try to lose ten to fifteen pounds over the next few months. Nothing drastic, but I think you'll be in much better shape if you'll take these few precautions. Also, no smoking."

"I understand." Bill stood and slipped on his jacket. "I want to thank you for your help, doctor. I know you're only visiting San Francisco, and I really appreciate your taking the time to see me."

Bernie shook Bill's hand and opened the door for him. "Please, think nothing of it, Not too many doctors remember anymore, but that's what we're here for."

Bill nodded and waved as he walked down the hallway towards the elevator.

Walking back to the desk, Bernie sighed as he thought about the thousands of people like Bill who tended to ignore their symptoms of impending ill health. Bill was fortunate that he had been apprised of his near serious condition in time to hopefully avoid a major problem.

Bernie had always taken pride in carrying out the Hippocratic oath he had repeated when he first became a doctor. He provided his services to the rich and the poor, with no charge to those who couldn't afford it.

He checked the time -- 6:15 p.m. He had reservations on a 8:30 flight back to Chicago and realized that he'd have to rush to get over to Al

Schottler's home for his luggage, say goodbye to he and his wife, and make it to the airport in time.

He knew this was probably going to be his last trip to the west coast. He had felt compelled to fly out and personally sever his previous obligations -- specifically his board position for the hospital in Los Angeles, and his volunteer work at the clinic in San Francisco.

As much as he hated to admit it, he had been easily replaced and was sure things would go on smoothly without him.

The plane took off and he took one last look at the Golden Gate Bridge before closing his tired eyes for a much needed rest.

Anne spent the entire day New Year's Eve getting beautiful. She washed and set her hair, gave herself a facial and manicure, and finally stepped into a hot bath, humming happily to herself. She couldn't even remember the last time she felt so warm and wonderful, and could hardly contain the excitement within her as she thought of the evening ahead. She closed her eyes and leaned back in the tub, letting the tiny bubbles tickle her chin.

She pictured Bill in his black tux and imagined him reaching out for her as she entered the ballroom at the party tonight. She smiled as she remembered the tingling feeling she had felt when he had held her -- even so briefly -- and found herself wishing it was time to leave for the party, so she could rush to his side once more.

On the other side of San Francisco, Bill sat on the edge of his bed, pulling on his black argyle socks and thinking about Dr. White's advice to him. He would do everything the doctor said, he told himself, and before long he'd be as healthy as ever. He just couldn't let himself be any other way now that he had Anne to think of.

"Annie..." he whispered her name softly as he pictured her lovely, smiling face before him. He had always known deep inside that he was attracted to Anne, not only physically, but also for her intelligence and delightful personality. She was such a wonderful woman, he found himself questioning if he was good enough for her. He stood up, slipped on his jacket and inspected his appearance in the dresser mirror. He shrugged his shoulders and smiled at his reflection, saying aloud, "We'll soon see."

He walked into the living room and poured a glass of club soda over ice. He resolved that tonight he would forget all the problems he had facing him at McDonald & Smith, and give his full attention to the one thing that mattered most to him now: Anne Maybury.

Anne had bought a long, slim-fitting black gown with a V-neckline edged with tiny glittering stones. She stood in front of the mirror, pleased with the perfect fit and happy to see she filled out the molded bustline appropriately. She picked up a gold necklace with a small black onyx dangling in a setting of tiny diamonds. Holding it up against her fair skin, she decided impulsively not to wear jewelry and placed the necklace back in her jewelry case. She laughed as she admitted to herself that the real reason was that George had given her the necklace, and tonight she wanted to feel free of all obligations.

Bill arrived at the ballroom only moments before Anne entered, when all eyes turned to stare at the beautiful woman they all knew as the "Assistant Vice President." For the first time in public, she wore her long hair flowing simply down over her shoulders, curling just slightly at the ends.

Several of the other men executives immediately approached her, offering their tables or a drink at the bar. Anne smiled courteously, while discreetly scanning the large room for the one person she came to see. Bill came up behind her, softly taking her hand and smiling broadly at the group of admirers surrounding her.

"Pardon me, gentlemen, but Mrs. Maybury promised the first dance to me, didn't you Anne?" He winked at her capriciously.

"But the orchestra hasn't started yet, Bill." One of the men interjected, slightly annoyed.

"Ah, yes, but I also have a bottle of Dom Perignon chilled and waiting at our table. Excuse us please." They walked away quickly, laughing and giggling like mischievous little children.

"Mmmm. It's absolutely delicious." Anne said as she savored the taste of the bubbly champagne tickling her taste buds.

"I'm glad you like it," Bill leaned over and placed his hand meaningfully on hers.

She raised her eyes slowly until she looked directly into his penetrating gaze. His grasp tightened as he felt that wonderful feeling coming over him again. He found himself wishing all the people around them would disappear so he could take Anne in his arms and never let her go.

Anne began feeling slightly dazed by the electric attraction toward the man across from her. "I ... I wonder when the music will begin..." she stammered, softly.

"I know a place where we can hear music all night long -- and we could celebrate the New Year alone..."

Leaving the nearly full bottle of champagne sitting on the table, they stood up and left the party, unnoticed by the growing throng of people around them.

Bill's contemporary penthouse apartment overlooked the shining bay of San Francisco and the busy nightlife below.

"What a wonderful view," Anne gasped as she looked out the large picture windows.

"Actually, it's a little too much for my taste. I'm basically a country boy at heart." Bill answered as he popped open a fresh bottle of champagne and walked over beside her. "My attorney found it for me after..." he hesitated only a second, "after the accident. He lives in the same building."

Anne nodded, and they walked over to sit on a large, overstuffed sofa in front of the crackling fire Bill had started upon their arrival. They raised their glasses for a toast.

"To the New Year," they both said almost simultaneously.

They sipped their champagne in silence, until Bill finally spoke quietly. "Annie, I think you know how I feel about you ... I mean, I've finally realized that you're all that I care about..."

"Oh, darling." She fell into his open embrace, and they kissed passionately, then tenderly. He held her closely, their pulses beating wildly.

Anne felt as if all the emotions she had kept pent inside were suddenly released. There were no barriers now -- nothing standing in their way. At that moment, she knew her long search for happiness and fulfillment had ended. "If only this moment could last forever." She wished aloud.

The crackling and hissing of the fire was the only disturbance to the silence surrounding them. Suddenly, the sound of firecrackers and bells rang out from the city outside. Bill glanced at his watch and reached for the champagne to refill their glasses.

"To 'us'." Bill toasted, holding Anne's hand firmly. They sipped their drinks and walked to the window, silently thankful they weren't out among all the thousands of partiers out celebrating January first.

Abruptly, Bill turned away from the window and walked over to the bar. Anne's dream world faded as she felt that same unwelcome air of tension building around them, and shuddered as she walked over to join him.

"Bill? What is it? Is something wrong?"

Bill stood tightly grasping the edge of the bar, staring down blankly. "I ... I think I had better take you home now..."

Anne took his arm, forcing him to look directly at her. "But why? What happened? A moment ago..."

"Please..." Bill interrupted, taking his hands in his. "Don't ask me to explain, because I can't ... I thought I was all through with this." He turned and walked back to the window. "Oh, sweetheart, I know I have no right to do this to you. Perhaps it would be better if you just forget about what happened tonight ... forget about me..."

"No." Anne said firmly. She paused for a moment and gazed tenderly up at the man she loved, then added quietly, "Whatever it is that's still bothering you can be overcome -- if we try -- <u>together.</u>"

Bill turned and pulled her tightly against him, hiding the mistiness in his eyes. "Thank you ... so much. I don't know what I'd do without you ... especially now."

CHAPTER FOUR

Dick sat is his office, trying to concentrate on the St. Peter's Hospital plans before him. For the last two months his life had seemed so confused -- he and Theresa rarely saw each other. She was away traveling more than ever, explaining that her superiors had given her extra assignments to fulfill. When they did see each other, it was as if they were strangers, not man and wife.

Dick knew he was also to blame, since he purposely worked late at the office or accepted dinner invitations from clients -- a policy he used to try to avoid. Tonight was the first evening he didn't have any plans in the last several weeks.

Since Christmas Eve, he and Julie had developed a detached relationship towards each other. She never mentioned the party or the kiss they shared so tenderly. Yet, they were very much aware of the uneasiness they felt whenever they were alone in his office.

Julie found herself fighting her inner desires in order to protect what was left of Dick's marriage. Dick too had to restrain himself from giving in to the temptation of an affair with Julie. He wasn't sure why he exercised this restraint since he certainly didn't have much of a marriage left, but he still couldn't bring himself to take that final step.

He seemed to be floating in a realm where he awaited some change in his life -- a change that would either renew his marriage or start a new life with someone else -- someone like Julie ...

At the same time in another part of the city, Theresa smiled as she waved to the group of salesgirls leaving the building. "Goodnight -- see you tomorrow." She turned and walked back to her office to pick up her coat and purse. As she approached the employee exit, she watched a happy, smiling secretary rush to greet her husband, who was picking her up after a long day's work. They walked briskly down the street, cuddling together like newlyweds.

Theresa's heart began to ache as she thought of the days so long ago when she and Dick had shared that kind of happiness. She almost wished they had never both decided on such demanding careers, despite the high salaries they received.

As she slowly drove through the heavy traffic toward their apartment, Theresa debated whether she should go to a restaurant to eat or stop and pick up a few things to make a meal at home. She was sure Dick wouldn't expect dinner at home, since their paths rarely crossed during the early evening hours anymore. She decided she didn't really feel like eating out, and pulled into the parking lot of a small market.

It was 7:30 by the time she reached their apartment. After changing into a comfortable caftan, she flipped on the stereo and began putting the groceries away. She didn't hear the front door open and jumped nervously when Dick approached from behind.

"Can I help?" he asked as he eyed the sack of food.

Theresa turned and leaned back against the counter, her hand resting over her wildly beating heart. "Oh, it's you."

"Were you expecting someone else?" Dick asked sarcastically as he walked over to the closet, taking off his coat.

Turning back to the refrigerator, Theresa replied, slightly annoyed, "Of course not. I just didn't expect <u>you</u> to be home at this time of the evening." Beginning to enjoy her accusatory edge, she continued, smiling slyly, "Don't tell me you ran out of <u>'clients'</u> to dine with?"

Dick decided to ignore his wife's obvious intention and casually pulled up a stool to sit nearby. "So how's everything at Magnin's lately? Still beating last year's sales rate?"

Theresa felt suddenly ashamed at her contemptible attitude and turned to face Dick, the churning feeling inside returning once again. "Everything's fine." She opened the refrigerator to put the orange juice away. "We're even beating our projections by a small margin." Shutting the door, she added, "How's the hospital going?"

"Slowly ... very slowly. But the Board seems to be happy with our progress, so I can't complain."

A heavy silence filled the room as they both searched for words to alleviate the tension in the room. Dick finally spoke up, offering, "Would you like a glass of wine with me?"

"Thanks ... that sounds good." She smiled sincerely.

As he filled her glass, Dick asked casually, "Remember that fellow on the Board I told you about a few months ago?"

Theresa thought for a moment. "Oh, yes, the one you said was such a nice guy."

"Yeah, well he's more than just a 'nice guy.' If it wasn't for his support at the Board meetings, we'd be in big trouble over all the unexpected delays. And now he's left the Board -- for some reason -- and I'm really going to miss him. He sure has a good outlook on life..."

Theresa suddenly knew she couldn't hold her feelings in one minute more and almost screamed, "What's happened to our outlook on life?" The tears began to roll down her soft brown cheeks. "We never talk anymore ... our marriage has turned into an 'arrangement' like the ones you read about. Oh, God, is it me? What have I done?" she pleaded, almost hysterically.

Dick grasped her firmly by the shoulders, shaking her slightly to gain her attention. "Theresa -- listen to me -- it's not just you -- it's me too. I guess we've both been going through some heavy changes the last few years."

Theresa pulled him close to her, resting her head on his strong, hard shoulder. "I don't want to lose what we had before. Maybe our marriage can never be the same as it was seven years ago, but I know we can make it better -- if we try..."

Dick held her quietly for a moment, then said softly, "I hope so too, babe ... I hope so too..."

Bernie lay staring up into the darkness, with Jenny sleeping soundly beside him. It had become increasingly difficult for him to fall into a natural slumber. His mind was always racing over the day's activities, only to end up dwelling on his impending death experience which was drawing nearer as each day passed.

He sometimes found himself contemplating the idea that his purpose here on earth might be solely to prove the life after death theory. He strongly believed in God and the fact that He gives each and every person something--or things--to accomplish during their lifetime.

A chill spread over his body as he realized the effect his experience might bring upon the entire civilization, should it be successful. "Could it be possible to end all of the senseless violence in the world?" he pondered to himself. The changes that might occur were impossible to imagine. He only knew he was developing an increasingly strong conviction that his life was in some way preordained -- that somehow he was destined to carry out a task that cold conceivably alter the ways of all mankind.

He sat up and swung his legs over the side of the bed.

Rubbing his forehead to try to ease a throbbing headache, he walked to the bedroom window and pulled the drapes to one side, gazing out over the sleeping city outside.

"Our Father who art in Heaven..." he whispered softly, his head bowed slightly. Repeating the Lord's Prayer slowly, Bernie gradually felt a warm, glowing sensation flowing over him. As he spoke the word, "Amen," he realized a wonderful new feeling of calmness had replaced all of his previous fears and apprehensions. He returned to bed, and promptly fell into a deep and restful sleep.

"Aren't you going to tell her?"

"Not just yet..."

Electra wasn't satisfied. "Why not? She has a right to know."

"I'm just waiting for the right time. And, besides, I don't know if I want to hurt her by giving her false hopes."

"What do you mean 'false' hopes?"

Rosamond realized the folly of her words immediately. "I should have said 'probable' hopes. You know as well as I do, there are too many variables to be absolutely sure of a successful outcome"'

Electra's feelings were quite apparent as she blinked into another dimension, leaving Rosamond alone with her own thoughts.

"I just hope I can count on Electra to guide me satisfactorily during my upcoming temporary transition ... especially since I will be just out of grasp of my universal knowledge bank..."

CHAPTER FIVE

A few weeks passed, and Bernie was called in more frequently to Gerry's lab for observation. He didn't need to be told that his condition was deteriorating rapidly, and the critical point was approaching fast.

Finally, the day arrived when Bernie knew his visit to the clinic would be a permanent one. He stood in his apartment, trying to memorize all of the parts of his life there: the simply framed works of art, the precious sculptures, the pieces of antique furniture that had decorated his parents' modest home. His gaze rested on the delicately framed picture which stood on the fireplace mantle with his other prized possessions -- the picture of a smiling, happy Jenny. He outlined her face with his finger, then decided on impulse to take the picture with him -- as if her loving smile could keep them bonded no matter what lay ahead of him.

Gerry had been in his office since early that morning, repeatedly going over Bernie's files without really expecting to read anything new. He also knew that Bernie had reached the stage where they would have to confine him for constant care, and how hard it would be for both of them from now on.

Just then Bernie walked in. "I hear you have excellent accommodations here, doctor?"

Gerry forced a smile and rose to shake his friend's hand warmly. "The best around -- and we only hire nurses with 'specific' qualifications, if you know what I mean."

Their tense laughter rang throughout Gerry's big office. Gerry opened the door and led Bernie down the hall to the elevator where they went to the third floor and found his room. Bernie was introduced to his nurse, a Miss Greenbaum, who seemed to indeed have a model's figure together with a pleasant personality.

"Now I know I'm going to like it here." Bernie teased.

"I'm glad, Dr. White," she answered sincerely.

"Please -- call me Bernie."

"Okay, if you'll call me Sharon. And now, if you'll please don the latest fashion in hospital-wear." She produced the familiar white smock from a drawer nearby. "I'll be back shortly with some reading material and lunch and dinner menus for your perusal." She smiled brightly and left the room.

Visiting hours were limited to two hours in the afternoon, and Jenny came to spend the entire time with Bernie. Upon her arrival the first day, she quipped facetiously, "So I see I have new competition already. Good grief -- a girl can't even trust her man in a hospital anymore."

Bernie played along good-naturedly. "Why, Jen, whoever are you referring to?"

"You know <u>very well</u> I mean that blond bombshell in a nurse's uniform they so graciously assigned you. I"11 have to talk with Gerry about this." She could hardly keep from laughing outrageously.

"Perhaps you should ... I confess I'm getting a little strained from continuously fighting her off. I guess I'm just irresistible, that's all..."

She pinched his arm playfully and sneered, "Oh you."

"Ouch. Cut that out or I'll have to ring for my nurse to administer some 'external' medicine."

They continued to laugh and joke and sometimes talk seriously throughout each visiting period, with Bernie trying in vain to hide his increasing pain and agony.

As the days flew by, Gerry prescribed some medication to relieve Bernie's pain, but another effect was constant drowsiness, and as a result, Jenny's visits turned more to quiet handholding than lighthearted conversation.

Then one day Gerry intercepted Jenny on her way down the hall to Bernie's room.

"Jenny -- I tried to call you at home early this morning..."

Jenny smiled and answered, "Oh, sorry Gerry, but I was out of the house extra early today because of some new RN's I had to break in this morning."

Gerry hated to have to ruin her happy mood, and hedged momentarily before continuing. Casually, he led her out of the middle of the hallway toward a staff lounge, where they sat down. All the while Jenny was looking at Gerry curiously.

"What is it, Gerry" Why all this mystery?"

Gerry decided to plunge right in. "We're doing a series of special tests on Bernie today, so I'm afraid he'll be unable to have visitors..." He saw Jenny's brows furrow and instinctively knew the next question, so he beat her to the punch.

After all, he told himself, she had to find out sooner or later. He placed his hand gently on hers and said "Bernie's not here just for the reasons he told you. He found out quite some time ago that his previous heart attack was compounded by congestive heart failure -- his only hope now is a transplant."

Jenny's impatience at being deterred from seeing Bernie was beginning to show as she interrupted abruptly. "You're not telling me anything I don't already know, Gerry." She started to stand up and gather her belongings. "Bernie told me all about his condition quite some time ago."

Gerry's hand came down gently but firmly on her shoulder, and the look in his eyes made Jenny shudder as she sat back down, slowly.

Gerry reached for her hand, grasping it tightly in his. Jenny's gaze never left his face, her eyes glistening from the onset of the tears she was fighting so hard to control.

"Jenny, you know Charley and I love you very much and wouldn't hurt you for the world. We introduced you to Bernie because we felt you would make such a beautiful couple... and, thank God, you have had a wonderful relationship together. So please believe me that everything we have done over the last few months has been with you and Bernie both in mind."

Jenny started suddenly, "You mean he'll recover?"

"I'm afraid not, Jen." He took a deep breath and made up his mind to tell her the seriousness of the situation.

"Jenny..." he felt almost awkward while trying to justify the future for her and Bernie. "Bernie's heart can't last more than a few more weeks -- at the most."

The last words seemed to sink into Jenny's innermost being, painfully cutting through her body like a sharp knife. "What's going to happen...?" she choked back the tears, feeling her throat convulse involuntarily, restricting her speech significantly.

Gerry went on, softly, "We're searching desperately for a transplant, but ... well ... you know how difficult it is to find an available and, more importantly, <u>compatible</u> organ."

She nodded, letting the tears flow freely down her cheeks now.

"In any case, " Gerry reassured her, "Bernie has agreed to submit to cryogenics, if necessary, to wait for a donor."

His last words came as a complete shock to Jenny. Of course she had studied the cryogenic theory briefly in medical school, but she found it amazing that Bernie, as conservative as he was, would agree to such an unorthodox method of self-preservation. Her thoughts were interrupted by Gerry, who spoke clearly and slowly, to make sure she would understand.

"I know what you're thinking, Jen, and believe me, we've done extensive research in the field, which is very favorable in the end result, or we would never have suggested it."

He contemplated his next words for a moment, and then added, "He's not only doing this for himself, you know. . . " He watched Jenny's subtle reaction as she raised her eyes to meet his. "He's agreed to help me try to prove the theory of life after death." He continued rapidly now. "Bernie hasn't much choice, remember that. He's dying and there's nothing we can do to cure him. We can lessen the pain, sure. There's just not another appropriate organ available for transplant yet -- that's all." He felt he was trying to convince himself along with Jenny that they were all helpless as far as Bernie's case was concerned. "So, we are constantly monitoring his physical state, and will instigate the most advanced cryogenic methods at the moment of his clinical death..." His voice cracked involuntarily, and they grasped each other firmly for support, as if their combined efforts could help them survive the emotional turmoil they both felt.

Minutes passed while they tried to calm each other down, thankful they were alone.

Jenny felt so drained of all feelings and emotions and so terribly confused, that she could hardly believe she had just arisen to start a new, invigorating day just a short time ago.

Gerry looked sadly at the small figure before him and wished he knew some magic words to cheer her up and make her forget all that was on her mind. Then, without a second thought, he said, "You know what? I think it would be a great idea if you would come and stay with us for awhile. After all, Charley has been after me for ages to get 'Aunt Jenny' over for an extended visit. And you know how grateful she would be to have some adult company for a change. I swear she's beginning to act like one of the kids lately."

He saw the beginning of a smile come across Jenny's face and let out a sigh of relief while waiting for her hopefully positive answer. He decided to add another incentive.

"Don't forget, we live ten minutes closer to town than you do."

Jenny decided on the spur of the moment to accept, wondering subconsciously if she would regret it later. "Okay, Gerry -- you talked me into it. But don't think I won't come and go as I please. After all, a visit is a visit. You know I love your kids and Charley ... but..."

Gerry raised his hands defensively, smiling. "Okay, okay. So we'll give you your own key, even."

Jenny leaned over and gave Gerry one of her sisterly bear hugs, whispering softly, "I don't know what I would do without you, honest."

"Don't worry, pal, the feeling's mutual. Just do me one favor during your stay, and baby-sit once in a while so Charley and I can re-establish our 'marital relationship'." She nodded and they both enjoyed the much-needed laughter that followed.

Jenny looked up at the clock on the wall and shook her head, reaching for her clipboard. "If I don't get going, I'll miss my rounds." She forced a half-smile and walked toward the door. "Please tell me everything, ok?"

Gerry nodded and took a deep breath, exhaling slowly, saying a silent prayer for the journey they were all about to embark upon.

Bernie lay in his hospital bed feeling totally constricted by the multiple tubes and wires attached to his body, which seemed to only increase the rate at which his mind was operating. Questions he knew there were no answers to kept infiltrating his consciousness, badgering his reasoning for even the slightest hope of a solution. But none surfaced, and he knew for the time being at least none would be forthcoming.

He had even lost interest in the teasing game he had established with his pretty nurse, a fact which mildly surprised him. She rarely came in now, except on direct orders from Gerry or one of the other specialists to perform some minor task, and even then they remained silent, with Bernie making it obvious he wasn't in the mood to speak to her.

It was only when Gerry came in that Bernie felt he was even remotely his old self again. Perhaps, he supposed, because he didn't feel at liberty to talk about his innermost thoughts to anyone else.

As if by cue, Gerry swung open the door and entered the room with the same broad, reassuring smile he had taken to wearing each time he visited.

"So, how's our star specimen this morning?" Gerry beamed.

"Your 'star specimen' is feeling lousy, if you really want to know," Bernie answered testily.

"Oh come now, Bernie, let's not let this thing get the best of us...

Bernie slowly, and painfully, raised himself up in the bed, adjusting the mass of tubeage attached to his right am. "Just suppose you tell me how in hell you would feel with all this garbage attached to you day and night?" He waved his free left hand back and forth across his torso. "Don't bother trying to tell me again how I was briefed on all this before checking into this place."

Gerry stood silently beside the bed, surprised by this sudden outburst. He knew how uncomfortable it all was, and he and Bernie had discussed it at length many times, as Bernie said, but Bernie had always been so level-headed and willing to accept the whole procedure that Gerry had not anticipated a negative outburst such as this. He was contemplating the best form of counter-attack when Bernie spoke, apologetically.

"I'm sorry, Gerry. I guess I just had to get it off my chest to somebody, and you just happened to be the lucky one. I knew this wasn't going to be easy before I agreed to it, and I realize the future is even more unpredictable. So just forget it, okay?"

Gerry was relieved, but concerned for his good friend. "Okay, pal, but are you sure you're all right? Just give me the word if the pain gets unbearable."

"No." Bernie interrupted. He realized he almost yelled his answer and consciously lowered his voice before he leaned back and closed his eyes, trying to relax. "I'm o.k."

Gerry looked closely at Bernie for any telltale signs of uneasiness. Bernie caught his concerned look and reiterated, "I'm fine, Gerry. Really."

Gerry nodded and pulled up a chair, pausing momentarily. "I may as well tell you that I saw Jenny this morning..."

Bernie stiffened noticeably. "You mean you didn't reach her by phone?"

"No I'm afraid not... she evidently had some new RNs to check up on this morning and left early -- before I could catch her. But we had a long talk, and I think she understands that the matter is pretty much out of our hands. I explained that I had advised you not to speak to her about your participation in the...'experiment.'" His eyes met Bernie's squarely and he said, "Besides, I'd like you both to try to be optimistic about the eventual outcome... I know I am."

"How did she take it?" Bernie felt an uncomfortable churning deep inside, knowing he most probably would never see her again.

Gerry sensed his feelings and said reassuringly, "She'll be fine, Bernie. And don't worry. You know it will be good for her to be occupied with the kids, and Charley and Jenny are such good friends." Bernie felt slightly relieved at hearing of this arrangement, although he feared Jenny's inquisitive mind just get the better of her, which could present complications as far as Gerry's research was concerned. But that was all in the future, and suddenly it was just too much for him to worry about at the moment.

Their silent thoughts were simultaneously jarred when a male nurse came through the swinging door holding his lunch tray with more of the unappetizing food he was trying not to get used to. Gerry stood up and smiled as he noticed Bernie's wrinkled nose and said playfully, "Oh, come now sir, do you dare to snub the fine continental cuisine we so graciously serve you this day?" In finishing the sentence, he bowed, lowering his clipboard formally.

I'll tell you one thing -- I've never in all my days as a physician prescribed such a pathetic excuse for food to any of my patients."

Gerry laughed and waved a silent farewell as he left Bernie to eat his lunch.

Bernie nodded and grimaced as he lifted the lid on one of the containers on his tray, displaying a sickly glob of cottage cheese with a wilted piece of parsley stuck haphazardly on top.

Bernie stared into the darkness surrounding him in the Intensive Care private room they had moved him to, concentrating his vision on the slit of light that filtered through from the hall outside, making its mark across the bare wall in front of him. There were no sounds to disturb his thoughts, since it was well into the early morning hours.

He tried closing his eyes once again, and slowly let his mind wander. He taught first of Jenny -- sweet, happy Jenny. He had thought so much about her during these long, lonely days and nights when he underwent test after test, until the specialists were satisfied with the results.

He deliberately forced his mind on to others he had met recently. There was Harry and his wife, Marion. A smile crossed his lips as he recalled their simple dinner together that had turned out to mean so much to him. Again, he found himself mentally repeating his desire to help them cope with their deep sense of loss over their beloved son, and hopefully achieve a happier relationship with each other. If only he had more time...

He thought of the new children's ward being constructed in Los Angeles at the St. Peter's Hospital and was inwardly proud to have been a part -- even if minor -- of approving the plans as a member of the Board of Directors. He remembered Dick Pearson. What an intelligent, bright mind he possessed. What potential he had for the future. Sadly, Bernie thought of the rumors of Dick's marital problems that had been voiced after the last meeting he had attended. He had never met Dick's wife, but somehow had a feeling that things could be worked out if only someone knew the answer. "What answer?" he asked himself silently. As usual, he felt mildly shocked and perhaps a little foolish when he realized he was practically carrying on a conversation with his own subconscious mind.

Suddenly, his mind flashed with pleasing clarity on his first meeting with Dick's secretary -- what was her name? Oh yes, Julie. What a catch she was going to make for some lucky man. Of course, he knew he had appeared more as a father figure to her, so it had been senseless to pursue the possibility of a relationship. He chuckled silently at his 'dirty old man' daydreams.

On the subject of attractive women, he recalled with pleasure his brief friendship with that beautiful black woman on the plane -- What was her name? He couldn't remember, and had misplaced her business card somewhere. With art inward smile, he decided that he'd introduce her to Dick if his marriage finally did break up. "That is, if I'm still around then," he reminded himself silently.

They all had so much to live for. Harry and Marion; Dick and his wife; Julie; and then there was Bill Anderson, the man he had examined as a favor to Al Schottler in San Francisco. Bernie was especially troubled whenever he thought of Bill. He knew the vague details about Bill and his wife's suicide, and Schottler had more than casually suggested that he thought Bill was interested in someone new, but was apparently too confused to straighten himself out.

It was almost ironic that Bill could be on the verge of a heart attack solely as a result of overworking himself senselessly, while Bernie lay here with a fatal heart disease and had never worked more than eight hours in any one day in his life. If there had only been more time to convince Bill how important it is to live life to the fullest while you have the chance -- a chance that so many don't even get. Bernie's mind worked feverishly as he cursed himself for not taking more interest in so many others during his lifetime. In reflection, he realized painfully how much more he could have done.

He fell into a troubled slumber, tossing fitfully until the first rays of light shone through the one small window in his room.

Two weeks passed, with Bernie's condition rapidly deteriorating. Gerry and his team began personal, around-the-clock supervision of the monitoring. Gerry tried as best he could to explain to Bernie as time passed the current state of his illness, but it soon became apparent that Bernie could no longer keep his mind at the appropriate level of consciousness to comprehend Gerry's words. Gerry knew the drugs that were being administered to limit the pain were the main factor in Bernie's fluctuating awareness of the world around him. They were still having no luck in locating a donor for Bernie, but never ceased in their constant search for a transplant.

Finally, Bernie lapsed into a type of unconsciousness similar to a coma, and Gerry knew the killer disease within him was getting close to achieving it's goal. Gerry began sleeping on the couch in his office at nights in order to be nearby when the time arrived that would spring him and his team into instantaneous action.

That moment arrived exactly five weeks after Bernie had been checked into the hospital. Gerry happened to be the one present when the EKG let out it's ominous unending beeping tone which indicated the heart was no longer functioning. He knew that efforts to start the heart again would be fruitless due to the nature of the disease, however, the team nonetheless went through standard procedure to revive the patient, more for the records than for the possibility of resuscitation.

At the same time, preparations were rapidly taking place for the immediate freezing of Bernie's body before too many brain cells were destroyed, even though advanced devices had been activated to try to minimize this precious loss. Each member of the team was moving frantically now, working against time, and so far they were exactly on schedule to the second.

Finally, after what seemed like hours of labor, but had in reality been only a matter of moments, the large dome was in place and the vacuum operating perfectly. Bernie's body lay still and quiet, gradually cooling down to the temperature that would be maintained indefinitely. The team monitored the digital readouts and dials encompassing the sophisticated computer, satisfied that everything was proceeding as scheduled.

Each of them had the same unanswered question underlying their intense concentration. Would they be as successful in reviving the patient even if an acceptable transplant was found? No one was sure, though they had gone over all the possibilities hundreds of times, looking for any small items they might have missed, and finding none.

The team settled into the prearranged schedule of taking turns monitoring the body. Gerry called Charley several times a day just to hear her voice -- she always had a calming effect on him. He was grateful she never asked questions about this project, especially since it involved their good friend, Bernie. She and Jenny knew only that it concerned cryogenics and she had been sworn to secrecy at that. Soon, he told himself, soon I'll be able to tell the whole world.

CHAPTER SIX

During those last days, Bernie's mind had not been as idle as all the doctors had surmised, although he couldn't seem to quite grasp whatever it was that Gerry was always trying to tell him on his frequent visits. No matter, he thought, and again let his thoughts wander to the innermost corners of his mind, dusting off many old memories that had long since been forgotten.

Time seemed to lose perspective to him, and he felt as if he were almost floating. "Oh yes, " he reminded himself, "it's the drugs." Then a moment later, "What drugs?" he asked. "Who cares," he answered himself, as he fell into a deep sleep. It was so very comforting to get away from it all ...

Suddenly, the pain in his chest was all gone and Bernie rejoiced as he enjoyed a wonderful floating sensation. Only this time it was more comforting than the drug-related release he had grown used to. He tried to think clearly as he focused his vision on the spectacle before him: his body lay outstretched on a bed below, a large dome covering him completely. Gerry and his team were running back and forth adjusting the equipment. Bernie was just about to interrupt the whole thing when he came to the shocking realization that he was watching from above. He had obviously left his body and was just about to investigate his new self when the lights faded abruptly.

CHAPTER SEVEN

Gerry had just arrived in his office when the phone rang. He let it ring just long enough to hang up his overcoat and then picked up the receiver as he sat down behind his desk.

"Dr. Silver," he answered automatically.

"Dr. Gerald Silver?" the raspy voice of a long distance operator asked on the other end.

"Yes?"

"Just one moment please," There was a pause and he heard her tell the other party to "go ahead please."

"Gerry?" A loud male voice boomed over the wire. Gerry immediately recognized the sound of his old friend's voice and answered, "Tony. Good to hear from you." Tony had attended medical school with Gerry and was now Chief Resident Surgeon at St. Joseph's Hospital in New York.

Gerry's pulse began to speed up as he anxiously hoped for the news they had been waiting for.

"We may have found your transplant for you. A young man in a fatal car accident -- his family has donated any needed organs and it looks like a perfect match."

Gerry was so excited he could hardly acknowledge Tony's last statement as his mind raced over the mental checklist of the events to follow if, indeed, this was a compatible heart. Finally, he managed to spurt out, "Tony. I can't tell you how thankful I am to you. And especially to the parents of the donor..." he hesitated a moment as he pictured Bernie's body in it's state of suspended animation, then added, "You see, this patient is a very close friend of mine ... (he couldn't bring himself to say "was", for obvious reasons).

"Just let me know how the operation works out, okay?" asked Tony.

"You bet." They spoke for a few more minutes, finalizing the transferal arrangements.

Gerry figured out that if all went smoothly, he would be in the operating room tomorrow at this time.

He picked up the phone again and asked his nurse to reserve the operating room time and notify the heart specialist who was to perform the surgery.

Thirteen days had passed before the transplant was located. The fourteenth day marked the beginning of the preparations for resuscitation, and each of the doctors checked and rechecked each and every step carefully.

Gerry felt the silence in the room grow heavy as the countdown continued. Slowly, the minutes ticked by. Finally, Bernie's body was ready for surgery, the temperature still maintained quite low, typical in many surgeries involving the heart. Gerry said a silent prayer that they would be successful -- let them bring Bernie back a cured and healthy man.

The heart/lung machine was instituted at precisely the right moment, providing the essential life support system to the newly awakened cells to hopefully prevent serious cellular damage.

The operation went flawlessly, and the Chief Surgeon surpassed himself in an effort to make this dream come true.

With the last sutures in place, all eyes became glued to the EKG (with the exception, of course, of the few physicians attending to the dressing of the incision). Finally, the crucial moment came when the life supporting apparatus was dramatically shut down as the injections were made to hopefully start the organs working normally.

"Come on Bernie... come on." Gerry whispered earnestly.

The first bleep on the EKG made everyone jump involuntarily, then the room was filled with a chorus of cheers, with everyone hugging each other, shaking hands and slapping backs. Despite their overwhelming feeling of euphoria, each member of the team set back immediately to the task now at hand -- that of going through the extensive checklist to verify that all was fine.

They had allowed a two-hour span for Bernie to regain consciousness as the surgical anesthetics wore off. When two and a half hours had passed, Gerry became nervous and everyone else became visibly concerned, each member mentally going over all of the stages they had so carefully carried out. There was just no reason for Bernie's extended state of unconsciousness -- at least no reason that medical science had yet discovered. A silent vigil was begun, with each doctor waiting anxiously for any sign on the monitors that might disclose the answers they were looking for.

"I'm still not sure I understand..." thought Bernie.

"Keep trying ... you'll grasp it eventually," answered the entity he had been speaking with for some time, who be was asked to refer to as "Electra".

She (or "he", as she sometimes appeared for Bernie's benefit) continued, using a tone much like Bernie remembered from his early school days when his teacher was patiently trying to get a particular point across. Electra now appeared as a middle-aged woman of medium height and build, conservatively well-dressed, and sitting demurely on an overstuffed sofa in front of him.

They seemed to be conversing in a room much like his den at home, paneled with a heavy oak, and with a desk and two large comfortable sofas facing each other in front of a fireplace. He looked around the room again and noticed many familiar appointments, together with several antiques he had once admired from afar but had never even dreamt of owning. The thought made him ask, "where are we?"

"As I tried to explain to you before, Rosamond, you always have the ability to be wherever you want to be. Therefore, what you see is an extension of your imagination and, of course, your 'desired' surroundings."

Bernie broke in abruptly, "And why do you continue to call me 'Rosamond' when my name is Bernie White? Dr. Bernard H. White." He repeated flatly.

Electra smiled casually, and looked toward the fire, which suddenly began to flare up in the fireplace. Bernie reflected on this momentarily, since, as he recalled, there hadn't even been any logs in the fireplacae a moment ago.

"'Rosamond'" Electra began kindly, "is the name you are known by at 'home,' or, if you please, by your limited understanding, a place you might call 'heaven'."

"Now I know I don't understand." Bernie felt completely lost and yet he had a compelling urge to find the answers to the questions that loomed endlessly before him.

"Okay, let's start over at the beginning again," Bernie said reasonably. "I remember being in the hospital and floating in and out of consciousness. Then I recall the point where I think my physical body died, since I felt a release from all pain, and found myself floating up above my body, witnessing the doctors below me and their activities. Then, all I remember is the lights going out, and...now...here I am... Talking with you about things and places and people I don't have the faintest understanding of." Bernie flopped down into the sofa opposite Electra, who at that point was fading and reappearing (much to Bernie's dismay) as the graying old man she had assumed the form of before. Bernie seemed to maintain his familiar Earth form, with the exception of his waistline, which he preferred to present as slightly less expansive than before.

"And why do you keep doing that?"

"What?"

"You know what. Changing your form from man to woman to man again. It would certainly seem that your existence is not very stable, from my point of view."

"And what is your 'point of view?'" asked Electra pointedly.

Bernie hesitated and then answered somberly, "I confess I really don't know anymore."

"Perhaps if you were to go back and reconstruct the research that you undertook most recently before leaving your physical body, you might find some of the answers you're looking for," offered Electra, who was maintaining the old man figure.

Bernie realized she was making a deliberate attempt to help him by being in the form of the old man, since he found it much easier to relate to him than to the younger woman she had been before.

Mentally, he appreciated her effort, since he so desperately wanted to understand what was going on.

"You're welcome," said Electra lightly.

Bernie was beginning to feel like this whole experience was just too deep for him to grasp, but went ahead and accepted the fact that they could easily transmit thoughts mentally. After all, that wasn't so new. Standing, he took her advice to try to reconstruct the knowledge he had gained regarding life after death before leaving his physical state.

"I researched the accounts of people who had been pronounced clinically dead and then were revived, or somehow lived to relate their after-death experiences..." he began tentatively.

"Go on..." encouraged Electra.

"After completing my research, I had a very strong compelling feeling that there was surely a 'life after death' in some form or another." He glanced at Electra, and she nodded, still in the old man's form.

"Knowing that I was to die shortly, I remember feeling very sorry that I had not done more during my lifetime for all of the people I could have helped in one way or another. I suppose that's one reason why I volunteered for the cryogenic suspension--" He hesitated momentarily, looking up at Electra, *"Of course you know about that..."*

"Of course," she answered simply.

"Well, I just thought that perhaps if there was some possibility that I could return with the help of a heart transplant at some future date, I would then be able to carry out my desire to help others...

"Anything else?" Electra's form was beginning to fade a little around the edges, which she abruptly corrected, presenting a clear image of the old man again.

Bernie shifted uncomfortably. *"Well, there is a rather selfish reason for my wanting to live again, and I suppose you know what it is.,."* He looked at Electra for some sign of acknowledgement, but received none.

"I was just beginning to realize that I was really falling in love again ... with Jenny ... when I learned that I was terminally ill. All those years after Ellen's death, I felt sure there would never be another woman I could care about in the same way I cared about Ellen." He paused a moment to sort out his thoughts. *"All of a sudden, it occurs to me that there might be a reason for my newfound feelings that corresponded with my learning of my disease."* He looked at Electra questioningly, but received only a silent nod in return.

He pictured Jenny with her smiling, happy face and suddenly – amazingly -- she was sleeping peacefully beside him. He could feel the *warmth from her body touching his, and marveled at her delicate features and her love for him emanating even now as she slept contentedly.*

He smiled and reached out to touch her face tenderly. She opened her eyes momentarily and murmured, "Oh Bernie -- I love you so much."

Then, suddenly, just as her mouth opened again to say something else, he was wrenched away and found himself back facing Electra, where he forced himself to gather his thoughts, speaking slowly, "I suppose .. I suppose it could be that I was on the verge of hurting Jenny very badly by telling her I was not the man for her. I had planned to do that just before finding out about the seriousness of my condition, which seemed to settle the matter for me..."

"But now... now I realize I was wrong all along. Ellen had always wanted me to remarry if anything ever happened to her -- just as I always told her the same thing about myself."

Bernie was so engrossed in his new outlook on the whole experience that he nearly didn't notice the figure standing beside the fireplace, casually observing the outburst he had just exhibited.

Bernie could hardly believe his eyes as he stared at the woman he had married at an early age and spent so many happy years with, standing so very close to him, smiling in the way she always did when she caught him off guard. She looked wonderful -- so young and vibrant -- just like she did when they had first married. He suddenly remembered his own aged portrayal and at the same moment realized he had somehow automatically changed his appearance to the same youthfulness he attributed to those years so long ago. Pleased with the transformation, he approached Ellen carefully, inwardly afraid she might disappear as fast as she had appeared a moment ago.

Their thoughts seemed to fly rapidly back and forth between them, as they both exchanged happy memories from the years they had

*shared together. There was no need to converse verbally, and Bernie
suddenly realized he had finally accepted this new mode of
communication.*

*Bernie could not pinpoint exactly how long this exchange had
gone on, but felt he now was much more at ease with his surroundings.
As he turned to see if Electra was still there, he felt a sudden burst of
warm, fragrant air brush gently across his face, and turned to find
Ellen gone. Amazingly, he was not too surprised, and settled calmly
back onto the sofa opposite Electra.*

"Thank you," he said sincerely.

"For what?" asked Electra teasingly.

*Bernie ignored her and instead savored the warm, loving
feelings that had been generated by Ellen's presence and their joyous
trip back over their lives together. He was unhappily snapped back to
the matter at hand when Electra said simply, "You will return, you
know."*

*Bernie remembered all he had read concerning reincarnation
and past and future lives before answering. "May I ask in what body I
will return and in what time? And will I be on Earth, or some other
Godly creation?"*

*Electra smiled knowingly. "It is good what is being written in
your present time on Earth. Much of it will serve as a basic
understanding of the future for those who can open their minds to the
universe and it's possibilities."*

*She continued slowly, deliberately letting Bernie try to digest
the enormity of it all. "As to your questions, you will be returning to
Earth to occupy the same body you so recently left. As to the Earthly
time differential, it will be about two weeks."*

*Bernie was beginning to feel like his mind was going in all
directions at once. One thing he knew for sure, and that was he was*

not ready to return -- not quite yet -- he had so many unanswered questions and theories to identify.

Electra had once again read his thoughts and answered, "You will not learn the answers to all your questions until you have entered your next dimension."

*She noted the confused state of Bernie's mind, and clarified her statement as best she could. "You will eventually learn that, basically, every soul has to pass through twelve dimensions before becoming a companion of the Universal God. This does not mean you have to be reincarnated twelve times; only as many as is required to learn the lessons necessary to your development. Therefore, my last statement means that not until you leave your last body on earth **permanently**, (she chose to accentuate the word) will all your questions be answered, or, I should say 'you will find the answers for yourself'. Of course, you must know that your lessons are never-ending, and that upon finding the answers to the questions that seem so important to you now, many, many new questions will arise to start you into the beginning of your next dimension."*

Bernie's mind was really flying now, but Electra gave him no chance to regain his equilibrium. "Just remember that you have chosen to return to your life on Earth for specific purposes, and you were chosen to effect a turning point in current beliefs on Earth by way of your reinstatement to a normal, healthy life after dying and being kept in an animated state for an extended period of time until a corrective measure could be taken.

"I have 'chosen to return' for specific purposes..." the words kept repeating themselves in his mind when suddenly he remembered his earlier admission about wanting to help others. To start out with, he could think of several people he knew personally. As he had done shortly before leaving his physical state, Bernie thought of his recent friends and acquaintances: Harry and Marion, Dick in Los Angeles, Bill in San Francisco.

He pictured Harry, unhappily escorting hundreds of people around town, day in and day out, only to come home to an unsatisfying home life. Bernie felt sure that Harry and Marion could lead a happier and more fulfilled life if only... if only they could let their son become part of the past and concentrate on the present and future instead.

Electra interrupted his train of thought, "You know he'll be going back soon."

"Who?"

"They boy you are thinking of. Your friends have mourned all these years and, as a result, have made their lives very difficult -- all as a part of their intended lessons. However, as you suggest, you can easily help them "grow" and thereby profit yourself in achievement of your goals."

"But how can I stop them from mourning the great loss of their only son?"

As he spoke, he again felt the presence of another entity in the room and turned to see a young boy smiling broadly at him from across the room.

"You're.,."

"Danny? Yes, Rosamond, I appear to you as my most recent physical state, that of a nine year old boy.".

After a moment of silence, Bernie said, "You'll have to excuse me for staring, but I'm new at this sort of thing and fit it a little, well...'disconcerting', to say the least."

"I understand" the boy answered simply, "I am pleased that you wish to be of assistance to my earth parents in your realm."

Bernie couldn't help but add, laughingly, "You certainly don't speak like a nine year old."

In answer, Danny faded rapidly and reappeared as a tall, handsome, dark-complexioned man of about thirty. His rugged features reminded Bernie somewhat of Clark Gable.

"This is one of my favorite appearances -- I used it in my third life: around the 1930's...

Not finding any appropriate questions to ask, Bernie remained silent, spellbound by the events unfolding before him.

"My name is Spiral, and you may call me such if you like."

Bernie nodded in understanding. Spiral began walking casually around the room, stopping here and there to examine an antique or work of art as he spoke.

"As Electra has told you, I will be returning to a new physical state soon, this time as a female. My life as I see it now will be tremendously involved with the future of the world at that point in time." Turning to notice Bernie's look of intensity, he explained "I plan to be a scientist who will contribute greatly to finding the cure to cancer."

Before Bernie could interrupt to ask a question, Spiral continued quickly, stepping closer to Bernie. "Of course, everything may change as I live my life and I may instead end up having to learn many other lessons as a result, a possibility one must face before embarking on a new physical existence." He replaced a marble statue on the mantle and continued. "But let us get back to our mutual concern -- that of Harry and Marion Kirby." He smiled as he let their Earth names bring back fleetingly pleasant memories. "You alone can convince them of the 'meaning' of their joint physical relationship. For we all know the thread of physical life is only a certain length, and their limited future years will soon be behind them.

"In any case, I will tell you that before embarking on their present life, they decided, along with me, to be my parents in one life, *my offspring in the next. So you see, I have only left them for a short time, and will soon share a physical existence with them once again."*

Bernie stared at the smoldering ashes in the fireplace, trying with difficulty to digest this new information. After a moment, he looked up to ask Spiral a question, and, much to his dismay, found him gone.

"He finds it difficult to remain stabilized for any length of time," offered Electra, "You see, he is still in the preliminary stages of development."

Bernie nodded, even though he knew he didn't quite understand. He was still thinking about Spiral when Electra reminded him softly, "You must not dwell on it, Rosamond. Doing so only clouds the mind, making the answers harder to see. There were others you were concerned about?"

Clearing his mind as best he could, he agreed readily, "Yes, I was worried about another acquaintance, Bill Anderson. His wife committed suicide and his blood pressure..." he stopped, as he realized Electra was obviously fully aware of the situation.

"Well, I just thought if I got to know him a little better, I might be able to help him stop feeling so guilty ... although I'm not sure he'll listen, since I never knew his wife... or the reason behind the tragedy..' Suddenly he asked Electra, "Do you think I could speak to her?"

She replied cautiously "I'm afraid not. I can only tell you that when one takes it upon himself to end the life that was given to him, and is therefore not his to end, he must truly comprehend the extreme seriousness of his act before progressing. For some, the truth is quickly arrived at, but for most it requires a long and painful journey within themselves before they clearly understand the meaning of it all."

"But then what of my friend, Bill? What can I tell him?"

"You must realize that he himself is responsible for his guilty feelings." She paused momentarily. "He must find the root of these feelings and then you may, in fact, re-educate him to understand again the true 'meaning' of life."

"You mean his troubles have nothing to do with his wife's suicide?"

"Let us say, simply, that this core of behavior lies much further in his past than his brief relationship with his wife."

Bernie was beginning to feel mentally exhausted when Electra spoke again, rising to stretch languidly.

"I am afraid we do not have time to speak of your other friends, but I assure you that the knowledge you have gained will easily suffice to help you accomplish your goals upon returning to your realm."

The pain in Bernie's mind seemed to become almost unbearable as he tried to comprehend all that was being told him. It seemed so very hard to grasp, and the harder he tried the faster the thoughts seemed to evade his consciousness. He found it terribly hard to concentrate -- it was as if he was suddenly weighed down and constricted from movement and free thinking. Finally, he gave up, and let his mind drift comfortably into the darkest corners of his being.

The Speakers surrounded Electra, their beautiful vibrations flowing lovingly around her.

"You have performed extremely well, Electra."

Overwhelmed by their compliment, she responded gratefully, "Thank you. I could not have done so without your help and guidance."

Dismissing her modesty, the Speakers went on to the subject at hand. "You must realize that Rosamond will remain in this transitional realm indefinitely,"

"Indefinitely?" Electra echoed unbelievingly.

"Rosamond, as her physical self, must gain the required knowledge on her own before she may complete the lesson successfully and accomplish this monumental achievement. We must not be overbearing with our assistance or her efforts thus far will prove fruitless in the end." They hesitated, then asked sol "Do you understand, Electra?"

"Yes ... I believe so."

Their universal love and faith in all that is abruptly enveloped them in a harmonious junction with the energy touching upon and mingling wonderfully with every fiber.

The nurse sat quietly reading a book beside Bernie's bed. He had been in a coma for 31 hours. She didn't even notice the sudden flickering of his eyelids as he struggled to regain consciousness.

Bernie strained to identify his surroundings, blinking his eyes rapidly to clear up the hazy form in the white uniform sitting across from him with a book in her lap. Slowly, his gaze circled the room and settled on the EKG apparatus directly to his left. The steady bleep ran reassuringly across the screen and, gradually, Bernie cleared his mind enough to recognize the same hospital room he had last remembered visualizing from up above in the corner of the room. He glanced cautiously to the very corner he occupied and saw nothing but the sterile walls of the room where they met with the corrugated tiles of the ceiling.

The nurse casually flipped a page of her book, and looked up automatically at the EKG to check the patient's heartbeat. Her eyes passed briefly over the form in the bed. She jerked suddenly, dropping her book to the floor -- Bernie's eyes were open and staring directly at her in an almost mocking manner. She ran out the door, calling to the nurse at the desk much too loudly, "He's awake. He's come out of the coma. Call Dr. Silver right away."

The girl picked up the phone immediately while the nurse and the two interns on duty raced back into Bernie's room and began checking him over without really knowing exactly what to do next.

By the time Gerry arrived, Bernie had completely reoriented himself to his surroundings and state of being. He felt extremely weak, however, and smiled only tentatively as his friend entered the room.

"Bernie." Gerry grasped his hand tightly. He felt the knot in his stomach lessen a bit as he glanced anxiously over the dials and screens nearby and saw that all was well, so far.

"We were afraid ... I mean, the heart has been functioning beautifully... and then you didn't ... well ... I'm just so glad to see you're back with us, pal,"

Bernie saw the tears begin to roll down Gerry's face and slowly turned his head from side to side, then murmured softly with a mouth that felt like it was stuffed with cotton, "Great to be back..."

The news of their accomplishment leaked out sooner than Gerry would have preferred, since he hoped to wait at least a week to ensure Bernie's ascent back to a health existence before making a public announcement. As it was, after a mere four hours had passed, the press was knocking down the doors to get the specifics about the remarkable case.

Gerry was forced to call a press conference immediately to satisfy the eagerness of the reporters. He found himself, as he entered the conference room, surrounded by attentive, seemingly over-zealous men and women, poised with pen and pad in hand, ready to run to the nearest phone to report their stories.

He took a deep breath and forced himself to remain calm, then read from the short speech he had worked so feverishly on less than an hour ago.

"Ladies and gentlemen, may I welcome you to our clinic, in order that you may tell the world of our proud accomplishment; that of restoring a man to a living, healthy human being after being declared clinically dead for two weeks." He paused to allow the flurry of whispers to settle down to silence once again. "At the point of death, we immediately suspended the patient, using cryobiological methods, and exactly fourteen days later -- having located a uniquely appropriate heart transplant to replace the malfunctioning one which caused his death -- we were successful in reversing the cryogenic process, performing the delicate surgery involved, and finally, ascertaining that the patient has regained consciousness with a perfectly functioning mind and body."

The shouting and questioning in the room rose to almost an unbearable level, until Gerry was able to regain a semblance of order.

He asked for individual questions and immediately was asked the name of the patient. Knowing that he could not hope to keep this fact a secret for long, he announced calmly, "Dr. Bernard H. White."

Again, several reports asked the same question simultaneously, the title of 'doctor' striking a coincidental note. "Was there a reason you chose a 'doctor' to try this on?"

Gerry answered that and endless other questions, all the while trying to remain as objective as possible under the circumstances. The last thing he and his superiors at the clinic wanted was to have the whole matter blown up into some freak experiment. Because of this, he continued to stress the general principles of their accomplishment: a patient was declared legally dead, frozen in a cryogenic state, then reinstated two weeks later to apply surgery, which ended in a successful heart transplant, restoring the patient to normal recovery, as of this date.

Gerry had an extremely difficult time breaking away from all the excitement within the clinic in order to finally call Jenny and Charley. Jenny was at her apartment watering her many household plants when the phone rang. "Hello?"

"Jenny. Good news."

She recognized Gerry's voice immediately and tightly gripped the receiver, finding her heart beating abnormally fast. The only thing she could say was..."Bernie?"

"Yes. Yes. He's okay." He was relieved that she hadn't heard the latest news broadcast. "The transplant was located, we reversed the cryogenic process, operated and -- he's fine – he's really fine." Gerry had deliberately not told Jenny anything about the transplant being found until he knew the operation was a success.

Jenny was crying uncontrollably now, still with a vice-like hold on the phone, as if she were afraid to let go for fear of losing touch with reality. "Oh Gerry. When can I see him?"

"What do you think I'm calling about? Get yourself down here right away. Your friend has been asking for you ever since awakening from his little 'dream-world'."

She wondered fleetingly what he had meant by that last statement, but was so anxious to see Bernie she hung up immediately and practically flew out the door to her car.

Upon arriving at the clinic, Gerry led her into Bernie's room, then quietly turned and left so they could be alone.

Jenny tiptoed up to Bernie's side, noticing his eyes were closed and afraid to wake him unnecessarily. She gazed lovingly over his features, looking for any new or different facial characteristics after his ordeal, but could find none. As a matter of fact, Bernie looked more relaxed and at ease then she had seen him in quite some time.

She was suddenly startled when his hand reached out for hers. She felt the warmth and vitality flowing through him to be willingly accepted by her.

Bernie was beginning to feel more 'alive' now -- just a few hours after 'awakening' from his coma state. He had no misconceptions, however, and knew it would be a slow and tedious journey to complete recovery, as would be expected with any major operation.

He found he tired extremely easily, and now, with Jenny at his side, he tried to remain as quiet as possible in order to conserve energy and hopefully prolong their visit.

Jenny, too, was obviously concerned with his well-being during these crucial moments, believing he had just undergone surgery within the last couple of hours. Gerry had chosen not to tell her about Bernie's extended condition of coma after the operation until he and his team were able to uncover the "cause and effect."

As a result, this first visit between Jenny and Bernie consisted mostly of sharing a common, silent closeness which neither needed to verbalize. Only fifteen short minutes had passed when Jenny saw Bernie's eyes begin to close, as he fought back the sleepiness that was rapidly overcoming him.

She turned away, hiding the thankful tears that rolled generously down her cheeks. Once again, she felt an increase in the pressure of their entwined fingers and suddenly heard the faint words "I love you" slip from Bernie's mouth.

As she looked back at his face, she saw that he had finally given into the restful slumber he needed for recovery, but now there was a peaceful smile on his lips.

Jenny sighed and settled down to begin her intended vigil at Bernie's side until he was completely well.

The step forward in medical history was significant enough to make the front pages of all of the national newspapers, with international coverage picking up fast. Gerry had immediately seen the need to appoint one of his assistants to spend all his time briefing the press, TV and magazine people who seemed to come out of the woodwork. In any case, the headlines of most of the newspapers were very similar:

"Doctor dies -- is frozen -- and comes back to life to tell about it." Or, "Life after Death is Proven. Prominent doctor is witness."

The clinic was very happy, of course, to receive all of this favorable publicity. Gerry, however, had the uncertain duty of telling Bernie just how much of a turmoil their "experiment" had caused.

He arrived early at the clinic and walked into Bernie's room to find him healthily gulping down a soft-boiled egg and milk toast.

"You look hungry."

Bernie ignored Gerry purposefully, and licked the remaining egg yolk from his fork. "I may be an invalid for the time being, but I would have thought you guys could have ordered something more substantial than this." Bernie chided, as he indicated the empty plate before him.

"Just because you're trying to beat the record for the fastest recovery after major surgery," Gerry teased, "doesn't mean you can order anything your heart desires -- excuse the pun. After all, we all know about your expensive 'gourmet' preferences when it comes to food."

They both laughed and Gerry realized how good it was to be back talking to and enjoying his friend after such a long period of uncertainty about the successful result of the experiment.

Abruptly, Gerry asked, "Bernie, if you feel up to it, I'd like to ask you about, well, about what happened after... I mean..."

Bernie smiled knowingly, pushing his breakfast tray to one side of his bed. "You mean after I 'died'?"

He had said it so matter-of-factly that even Gerry, who had lived through it with Bernie, found it hard to accept rationally.

Bernie continued slowly, summoning all of his recollective powers to the surface. "I remember," he began tentatively, "the way I felt while under heavy sedation towards the... 'end'. I say the 'end' because soon after, I remember distinctly feeling an instantaneous release from all pain and a sensation of floating..." He noted Gerry's concerned face, then confirmed confidently, "Yes, Gerry, I said 'floating' -- somewhere up above you and the others as you tried to revive me." He grinned and added, "You almost make me feel sorry I had the same common experience as all your other clients."

Bernie's mind still seemed like a cobweb of unclear memories, but he strained to clarify what had happened next.

"I was just beginning to realize what was happening, when --all of a sudden -- all the lights went out. It was completely dark." He closed his eyes in an effort to remember more. "That's it. I can't remember a single thing after that until I opened my eyes to see the nurse sitting watch over me in ICU."

Gerry sat quietly reflecting on Bernie's words for a moment, then smiled and said, "Well, at least your story correlates with most of the other after-death reports -- even if you didn't experience quite as much as some of the others."

"Sorry to disappoint you..." Bernie replied thoughtfully. "Maybe something more will come back to me."

"Don't preoccupy yourself, Bernie." Gerry quickly inserted. "The main thing we've accomplished is a successful operation on a clinically dead patient after two weeks in a cryogenic state. The 'after death' theories should have enough credence as far as I'm concerned."

Bernie wasn't about to accept Gerry's apparent brush-off of all his 'life after death' research.

"You don't fool me, Gerry -- and you should know better than to even try to. I admit we've made a major accomplishment, don't get me wrong, but I'm also sorry I didn't provide you with more information to support your work."

"Look Bernie," Gerry interrupted, "you **did** die, and you were revived with a successful operation after two weeks. In actuality, you're living proof there can be 'life' after 'death'." He smiled pointedly.

"We're not speaking literally, and you know it." Bernie scolded. "Anyway... perhaps we may shake up a few people who believe 'once you're dead, you're dead.' After all, its obvious that my 'soul' evidently stuck around during my stint in the deep freeze." Bernie looked quite proud of himself.

Gerry shivered involuntarily at Bernie's casual reference to the cryogenic suspension they had employed, and marveled at his friend's ability to be so detached from it all. Finally, he added, "Well, we have no control over the public's reaction to this. Which reminds me of one of the reasons I came in so early today --"

Bernie looked at him quizzically as Gerry stood to walk over to the window to adjust the shades. "I haven't told you about the reporters and the extent of their coverage until now, since I didn't want to excite you."

"You mean I'm a national hero?" Bernie asked with mocking sincerity.

Gerry nodded slowly and then added, "Maybe even international.' Bernie was thoughtfully quiet for a few moments while he digested this new information. It was true he hadn't really dwelt on what might be the public's reaction -- or how he himself would feel as a result of it.

Gerry's next words answered many of his questions. "The press was very thorough, in most cases, and you made front page headlines ... at least for a day, anyway."

Bernie shook his head, disbelieving that such a major medical achievement would receive such limited interest. Before he could verbalize his thoughts, Gerry went on, his own disappointment very evident now.

" It seems that it will take several more successful cryogenic operations before the world will be ready to accept what we've done and what it could mean. Oh, there are those who have been profoundly affected, but unfortunately the skeptics far outnumber the believers. There's already an investigation in progress looking for some hint of a fraud."

"Fraud. Why, that's ridiculous." Bernie stormed. "After all the painstaking documentation we did to eliminate any questions of authenticity..."

"That's just the point, Bernie," Gerry interrupted. "Our foes contend we were too careful -- or too perfect -- in our preparations. As if in perfection lie guilty intentions.

"Anyway," he went on, holding his hand up to silence Bernie when he would have voiced further outrage, "after thinking it over, I've decided this type of opposition was inevitable. And as I said before, after several more successes, the people will have to believe us.

Of course, I admit privately to you and my colleagues in this venture that I did have high hopes of your not only surviving the physical aspect, but of your ability to document in detail ... " he paused, unsure of how to express himself, then smiled and said pointedly, "your soul's activities, if any, during those two weeks."

They both laughed over his bluntness, then Bernie replied, "Maybe there weren't any 'activities'...or maybe we're simply never to know about them while we're alive ... or, maybe ... although I doubt it, our adversaries could be right and there is no life after death."

"Now don't you get skeptical on me too, for Heaven's sake." Gerry scolded. "What about the common experience of floating above the body? Even you felt it. There's no other explanation that I know of except that some part of you exists after you die. And I haven't even mentioned all of the other unexplained phenomena that support the theory."

Bernie chuckled, then broke in, "Sure seems like I've heard this all before, somehow. You know I'm the first to believe in the survival of the soul ... say. Pretty catchy, eh? I'm a 'soul survivor.'"

Slowly, Gerry's face broke into a smile, then a laugh. "O.k., you nut, I ought to know better than to try to lecture you. It's just so darned frustrating to be so close to something really phenomenal and not be able to get the proof we need to satisfy even the weakest skeptics."

"Don't worry, Gerry. If it's meant to happen, it will. In the meantime, there's always the possibility that I'll still remember something."

"I agree," Gerry said with a grin. "After all, it's the least you could do after all the trouble we went through."

"Thanks a lot, pal."

Their relaxed camaraderie returned once again to relieve the tension in the air. As Gerry went towards the door to leave, he quipped, "By the way, your 'fame' with the press was overshadowed the next day by much more important events, such as the President's daughter's wedding--and one man's consumption of ten gallons of beer in five minutes -- things like that. I'll see you later, 'soul survivor'."

As the door swung shut, Bernie was laughing at Gerry's jovial comparison of events the press gave equal importance to. After a moment, though, he began to experience a sense of apprehension toward an unforeseeable future.

There was really no doubt that the use of cryogenics would now flourish around the world. People with incurable diseases who had the necessary resources would flock to newly built 'cryogenic clinics' for their bid at a future cure.

Unfortunately, only a very few (other than those connected with the medical profession) seemed to realize the greatest significance: that of Bernie's regaining his original personality and mind along with his physical stability.

That night Bernie had a hard time falling to sleep. The sedative he had been given earlier was apparently not effective enough to overcome all the thoughts that were constantly racing through his mind.

He seemed almost disoriented as his subconscious flashed memories back and forth, spanning the past up to the present. Finally, his exhaustion after the day's events and his mind's over-stimulation overcame his wakefulness and he slipped into quiet slumber. He felt the same floating sensation as when he was leaving his body at the point of death. This time he reveled in the feeling of weightlessness and the material restrictions which melted away.

He was back in his den, sitting behind his favorite desk, and enjoying the fire which was spreading it s glow throughout the room.

He was distracted from his peaceful relaxation by the figure who was stretched comfortably across one of the sofas in front of him, using the coffee table as a footrest.

"At least you could have the good manners to take your shoes off." He smiled as the shoes disappeared, leaving only the soft socks underneath resting on his table.

"So you can't even allow an old man some simple pleasures, eh?"

Bernie smiled and answered confidently. "You know how they say that we profit from the lessons we learn in our physical state? Well, I was taught at a very young age to take my shoes off before putting my feet on the furniture."

Electra deliberately changed into her "woman of the world" figure before answering. "Then you've obviously learned something,

*I'm glad to see," she said sarcastically, as she stood and walked over
to the desk to brood.*

*"However," she continued pointedly, "I might add that all that
you have yet to learn far outweighs your very limited present
knowledge."*

*Bernie again felt overwhelmed by this unpredictable feminine
figure, a feeling which resulted in his immediate defensive reaction.
"How can I learn when I don't even understand what's been happening
to me?"*

*Electra was silent again, employing her favorite method of
teaching others to find the answers within themselves.*

*"It's all so confusing..." Bernie began, "I can't seem to recall
any of our discussions when I'm awake, and yet I know how important
it is that I learn from my experiences, and profit from them."*

*He waited expectantly for her reply, and finally she responded
evenly, "You will remember..." She spoke as if another entity was
giving her instructions or the "authority" to continue. "It is not meant,
however, for the entire world as you know it to benefit from your
knowledge – at least not yet. Therefore, you will only be allowed to
speak of some of your experiences with us 'here at home,' and even
then only to the degree that-it will help mankind at the moment of your
time involved."*

*Bernie was not at all sure he understood this conversation and
was about to ask for more specific answers when he felt a sharp,
jarring sensation, followed by the words,*

*"Dr. White?" Again, and more forcefully this time, Bernie felt
the grasp tighten on his arm while the voice repeated, "Dr. White?"*

He slowly lifted his eyelids, already prepared for the vision in white
standing beside him, smiling broadly.

"We're ready for our next sleeping pill, aren't we?"

Rather than argue, he nodded and swallowed the pill, turning his head to make it clear he was intent on sleeping and simultaneously excusing the nurse.

After he heard her rubber-soled shoes pad out into the hallway and the door swing shut, he opened his eyes momentarily and scanned the room. Yes, he assured himself, he was here in the same room he had occupied during his entire stay at the clinic. Then why, he mused, did he keep remembering his den at home -- had it been a dream?

The sleeping pill soon had it's intended effect, and Bernie gave in to a peaceful sleep, slipping deep into the inner layers of his subconscious mind.

Jenny awoke in the middle of the night in a cold sweat, trembling from the dream she had just experienced so realistically. She rubbed her forehead and pushed the damp hair back from her face as she reassured herself it was only a dream -- the same confusing one she had experienced so often lately.

Awake now, with the light on beside her on the nightstand, she tried to analyze the dream she remembered so vividly. She seemed to be in some other time or place, with people she didn't really recognize. They were all conversing as if old friends, and then, the most disturbing part to Jenny, she would visualize Bernie.

As soon as she saw him, everyone else disappeared and they were alone, but in some totally different place. And what always frightened her after awakening was the fact that he didn't recognize her. She could never exactly pinpoint the reason why, but in her dream it didn't seem to matter -- and they would talk casually, although she could never remember what was said when she awoke.

She had been having these dreams for over two weeks now, and was becoming concerned as to their significance or meaning -- if indeed there was any. She didn't want to tell Bernie about them ... not just yet. It might upset him unduly. And she really didn't have anyone else she could turn to who would understand -- unless, of course, she employed a psychiatrist to help her interpret her dreams -- a thought which she scoffed at and considered a last resort.

As she reached over to turn out the light and settled comfortably back down on the pillows, she again visualized another experience that had bothered her and tried to explain realistically what had happened and why.

She closed her eyes and remembered the night when she had been sleeping and had opened her eyes (in her dream, she thought) to see Bernie lying close beside her, reaching out to touch her face loving*ly*. She had felt so wonderfully happy to see him and be near him. She had murmured the words "I love you," and then realized as she spoke, she was, in actuality, alone in her bed. Bernie was in the hospital. Not here with her.

She remembered starting to gasp with sudden recognition of her surroundings and the apparent apparition that had now disappeared -or she thought he disappeared -- but then, she really wasn't even sure what she saw ... or thought she saw.

But of one thing she was sure. And that was the overwhelming feeling of warmth she had felt. She knew that Bernie had been very, very close to her, even if it was in her dream. That was a fact she would always be sure of, no matter what anyone else tried to tell her.

Dick had gotten in the habit of arriving early at the office, which enabled him to sift through the previous day's work, make notes on any significant happenings for the day, and finally, to sit back and read the morning L. A. Times as he sipped his second or third cup of coffee.

Subconsciously, Dick knew that the real reason for his extreme promptness was to keep his morning contact with Julie to a discreet minimum, having already set up the day's activities for himself. Julie seemed content with this arrangement also, and their conversations were generally brief, to the point, and always businesslike.

Propping his feet up on the corner of his desk, Dick scanned the morning's headlines casually, until his gaze froze upon reading: "MEDICAL MIRACLE PERFORMED IN CHICAGO." Quickly, he read on through the text, which covered three columns and continued on to the next page.

Dr. Bernard White, a prominent Chicago physician for many years, recently succumbed due to a fatal heart condition. By previous agreement, which was kept secret from the public, Dr. White arranged to participate in an experiment never equaled before in medical history.

At the moment of his death, Dr. White was placed under cryogenic suspension, more commonly known as the technique by which the body is frozen in order to preserve all the organs and cells intact until a cure is discovered, at which time the body would be reanimated and, presumably, brought back to a healthy existence.

This technique has been used in several dozen cases to date in the United States. However, until now, none of the previous cases have been reanimated and/or cured.

In this case, when a compatible heart transplant was located for Dr. White, his body was quickly reanimated and the operation completed. Now, for the first time in history, a human being has been revived to a healthy state two weeks after he was declared clinically dead.

Is this proof of 'life after death'?

The article went on to describe Bernie's current status in postoperative intensive care. His progress had been most satisfactory, in fact many considered it remarkable. The doctors involved in the experiment were named, and brief descriptions of their medical background given, citing Dr. Gerry Silver as the major impetus of the project.

Dick's mind reeled as he tried to comprehend what he had just read. Carefully, he lay the paper down and stood up to look out the window overlooking the same people coming and going seventeen stories below that he had become so accustomed to seeing every day here at work.

This was the same Dr. Bernard White who had sat in his office casually examining his work. "No one would ever have guessed he was suffering from a fatal heart disease," he said aloud. Dick wondered momentarily if Bernie was even aware of it at the time they had met ... and yet it seemed that he must have been if he had agreed beforehand to participate in such an advanced experiment.

His mind raced forward, trying to cope with the new horizons that would automatically rise as a result of this momentous achievement. At this second, all of his architectural designs and drawings seemed extremely insignificant to him. This was a human life being experimented with. What really impressed him was that he had known and spoken to this man only weeks ago. He had to face the fact, perhaps more realistically than others, that a physical entity had died and been 'reborn'.

Dick began pacing the office, rapidly scanning his childhood upbringing and inbred beliefs. He had always been taught that if he wasn't good, he would have to repent for all the sins he committed if he expected to go to Heaven. Now, as he thought about his convictions for the first time in many years, he realized that he really didn't know what he believed -- because, truthfully, he was never overly concerned one way or the other.

His mind flashed over the more recent years of his life. He had been continually struggling to achieve -- trying to reach that untouchable goal -- not for himself as much as for others: his parents, his friends, and yes -- most of all , for Theresa. His vision blurred as the obvious truth hit him smack between the eyes. He had been knocking himself out all these years for all the wrong reasons. "Why?" he asked himself incredulously. No answer was forthcoming.

Perhaps his career was all a mistake from the beginning. He realized now that he had felt pressured to excel in a noteworthy occupation and so had chosen the field of architecture. If he could do it all over again, he asked himself, would he have chosen another profession? No ... he would still have picked his current vocation. At least he felt somewhat reassured to realize that. But to have driven himself mercilessly because of nonexistent expectations on the part of those around him.

Suddenly, he wondered if he would be where he was had things been different. There was really no way to know ... only useless speculation. His thoughts turned to Theresa. Perhaps she never really showed any preference regarding his field. He couldn't seem to remember now. He only recalled his own burning desire to prove his could be the breadwinner -- in a big way. Yet even now with his success, she still continued to work - and their marriage was a mess on top of everything else.

Wearily, he sat down, dropping his head down on his arms, feeling mentally exhausted after the 'awakening' he had just experienced. It all seemed such a waste of time...valuable time ...

Suddenly, he made a decision. He wrote a note to Julie and taped it to her keyboard in an obvious spot, then headed for the elevator. The note read simply: "Am taking a week's vacation -- RP."

Theresa had feigned sleeping in that morning, telling Dick as he dressed for work that she was taking the morning off after working late the previous night. As soon as she had heard the front door shut and the lock click, she had propped herself up in bed, lit a cigarette and dragged heavily, letting the smoke float out slowly through her nostrils before exhaling completely. Casually, she flipped on the nearby clock radio and relaxed, listening to the soothing music circling the room.

Their life lately had been a series of "ups and downs," with the bad times rapidly outweighing the good. The New Year had brought a new surge of warmth and excitement into their lives due to their previous "separation of ways" and things had seemed to take a turn for the better -- for a while.

Then, almost predictably, they slowly lapsed back into their previously incongruous life of double executives, each trying, halfheartedly, to maintain a semblance of peace in the home by forfeiting a trip or business meeting now and then.

Her daydreaming was abruptly interrupted with the hourly news report, which she listened to without really hearing. She didn't even pay attention to the announcer's raised tone of voice in obvious excitement proclaiming: "Dr. Bernard White's medical accomplishment" and, finally tiring of the tirade of verbal abuse spewing from the speaker, she twirled the knob to another station featuring nonstop music, even if it wasn't quite as mellow as she would have preferred.

She had just settled down again with her second cigarette hanging precariously from her lips, when she saw a shadow move across the wall towards the bedroom.

She clutched the blankets to her breasts and ground her cigarette into the ashtray on her nightstand, feeling her heart beating almost audibly in her chest.

The gasp of relief she exhaled when Dick entered the room was evidently unnoticed by him. He stood silently in the doorway for a moment before speaking, then said simply, "Hi."

"What ... what are you doing home?" Theresa stammered, trying unsuccessfully to camouflage her surprised tone of voice. She released her grip on the blankets and all too casually let them fall to her lap.

Dick walked slowly, purposefully, over to the bed and sat down next to her, clasping her hands in his.

"We have to talk..." he began.

"Is something wrong at the office?" Theresa asked immediately.

Dick smiled at her expected response and became even more confident in his intended course of conversation.

"No ... no, everything is fine at the office. In fact, now that you mention it, things are far better than I ever could have expected them to be." He smiled broadly to an uncomprehending Theresa.

"Then what..."

He stopped her before she could complete her question and asked, instead, "You're going to the East Coast this week, didn't you tell me?"

She nodded, her mind in a complete state of confusion.

"I'm going with you. And on the way, we-can stop in on a friend of mine in Chicago.

"But. . . "

He lifted his fingers to her lips. signaling silence, and for the first time she realized his proud, new dominance over her plans.

"I know you're scheduled to fly directly to New York, but we'll leave a day early and stop over there." He hesitated momentarily to make his point, "It's important."

Marion stopped at the church to drop off the chocolate chip cookies she had baked for the upcoming charity fund-raising event that her church sponsored each year at this time.

As always, she stepped into an empty pew to say a simple meaningful prayer, blessing her lost son Danny, and her husband, asking forgiveness for all their sins and shortcomings in life.

As she stood to leave the church, she again felt the same overwhelming warmth spread over her body that she had experienced several weeks before. It had happened when she had knelt in prayer at home one day when feeling particularly despondent over her life and, as always, the loss of their son.

She stopped and marveled at the unusual feeling for a moment and then, as fast as it had appeared, the warmth dissipated and she turned to leave the church.

She walked the familiar six blocks to their apartment, stopping suddenly as she overheard the paperboy on the corner shouting loudly'. "Read all about it. Dead man returns to life. Read all about it."

Without thinking, she rushed across the street and pressed a quarter in the boy's hand, taking a paper in return. She walked slowly back to her building, while reading the story behind the boy's selling line.

Harry arrived home as usual in the same rotten mood he had displayed every night for the past several years. He didn't even notice his wife sitting silently on the couch in the living room until he had hung up his coat and hat and called "I'm home." while heading for the TV.

He stopped short as he saw Marion staring into space with the newspaper on her lap.

"Hey -- what's the matter with you? You look strange -- like you're in a trance or somethin'." He shook her shoulder slightly, jarring her to attention.

"Oh ... Harry ... I..."

He could see she was obviously upset and sat down beside her, feeling slightly concerned over her unusual behavior.

"What is it?" he asked with genuine concern.

"I ... this article ... it's Dr. White," she sputtered and then began to cry quietly as she released the paper to her husband.

Harry read the article without commenting, and then stared straight ahead, letting his thoughts run unhindered through his mind.

He knew without thinking why Marion was crying -- the same reason this article was upsetting him. Their friend, the kind, reliable doctor of medicine they had grown to know and love, had unexpectedly proven there can be "life after death".

Their minds reeled simultaneously past all the projected meanings and possibilities this achievement offered. But, somehow, it all seemed so closely related to them. For some reason, though, neither of them could speak of, or put their finger on it.

Little did they realize on that particular day how wonderfully significant this news would be to them and their future lives.

Bill didn't immediately recall his relationship with the now world-famous doctor who had participated in one of the most significant experiments in medical history.

Not until his secretary called his attention to the fact that the doctor had made frequent trips to the West Coast did he suddenly remember the man who had so drastically influenced his life and behavior when he had been threatened with a heart attack, adding valuable years to his life.

He called Dr. Schottler right away and confirmed the fact that this was indeed the same Dr. White he had seen not so long ago. As he replaced the receiver, the intercom buzzed and his secretary announced Anne's presence outside and her request to see him. He rose immediately and went to open the door, smiling as he ushered Anne over to the conference area at one end of his office.

She and Bill had continued dating infrequently since the New Year's Eve party, both of them being ever cautious not to cross that imaginary line leading to a more involved and permanent relationship until Bill felt he could do so. They enjoyed each other's company and Anne seemed content with the present arrangement until Bill felt secure enough to offer something more.

One thing had changed in Anne's life, however. She found she no longer enjoyed her casual dates now and then with George. She had told him, much to his dismay (and his mother's delight), that she would not see him anymore.

As a result, she filled her solitary evenings reading and catching an occasional movie, not to mention the many nights she worked late at the office.

"And to what do I owe this unexpected pleasure?" Bill teased lightly. "I thought we solved all the company's current problems at yesterday's meeting."

She played along with him and answered suggestively, "Who said this was a business-related visit? I'm entitled to some break time once in a while too, ya' know."

Laughing at each other's antics, Anne walked over to pour them some fresh coffee. "So tell me something new and exciting," she said over her shoulder.

Bill hesitated before answering her question. He was thinking of the newspaper article he had just read. "Have you seen this?"

She glanced briefly at the paper and shook her head, handing him his cup of coffee. She sat down and read the article quickly.

"That's really something. It's amazing -- all the new medical advances being made."

They were silent for a moment and then Bill said suddenly, "I know him."

Anne searched his face for an indication of the extent of their acquaintance.

Then he continued, slowly. "He's the doctor that warned me about my high blood pressure. I owe a lot to him. His advice may well have prevented me from having a serious heart attack."

Anne remained quiet, and after a moment he took a deep breath and said, "Anyway, I'm glad that he survived. He's a great person and I was thoroughly impressed by him -- even in the short time we talked together."

The sound of the buzzer on the intercom interrupted their conversation and Bill walked over to his desk to receive his secretary's message.

Seeing that he was busy, Anne rapidly drank the last of her coffee and walked towards the door, smiling warmly at Bill. "Oh well, it was a nice 'break' while it lasted."

"Wait a second." Bill called back to her. "How about dinner tonight? I've been meaning to call you..."

"I'd love to. See you at seven?"

"On the dot."

As he watched her close the door behind her, Bill looked down at the message he had just received. It read: "See H. Smith at his home - one hour." Without thinking further about what Smith would have to say to him, Bill picked up his briefcase and left the office.

Hamilton Smith, Sr. sat in his favorite recliner next to the window overlooking his beautiful garden. He conducted most of the company's business from his home now, going into the office only when it was absolutely necessary.

The months that had passed since he announced his retirement had weighed heavily on him. Now, already nearing the end of June, he had still not made the expected announcement about his choice of a successor. The fact was, he admitted to himself reproachfully, that he had not yet made up his mind.

He had the usual pride and devotion towards his one and only son, who would someday inherit his vast estate overlooking the bay, together with over twelve million in other assets. But there was just no way he could ignore or excuse his son's arrogance, deceitfulness, and disrespect for the company he had worked so many years to build.

It was true that Smith Jr. put up an admirable facade at meetings (those he chose to attend infrequently, that is), feigning genuine interest of the matters at hand. But Smith Sr. hadn't gotten where he was now by falling for every obvious trick in the book.

That left Bill Anderson. Intelligent, well qualified, and hardworking.

Reaching for his tobacco, he refilled his pipe and lit it, the billows of white smoke swirling majestically up above him. What was it that made him hesitate? Why hadn't he chosen Bill long ago?

The same answer came forth: Bill worked too hard. As strange as it seemed, that could really be a problem. He had seen too many overly enthusiastic men work themselves into a nervous breakdown or a heart attack. And Bill was heading in the same direction.

Dismissing his thoughts for a moment, he turned to admire his collection of rose bushes bordering the narrow walkway through the garden. He noticed one particular plant that needed tending and was idly dwelling on it when he heard a soft rap at the door.

"Yes?"

His secretary stepped halfway through the doorway to announce, "Sorry to disturb you, sir, but Mr. Anderson is here to see you as requested."

"Have you located my son yet?" He asked hopefully.

"No, I'm afraid not. He neglected to leave word where he could be reached after leaving Monaco, sir..." She waited for a moment, then added, "I could try again, if you wish..."

"No, no ... never mind. Send Bill in. And bring in some cognac please."

Bill entered briskly and accepted the chair across from the President. After pouring their cognac, the secretary left the room quietly just as Smith Sr. began the conversation.

"Glad you could make it over Bill. I know it interferes with your work schedule to ask you to come way over here."

Bill shifted uneasily in his chair. He was not sure about the nature of this unusual meeting, and was at a loss as to how to proceed. "It was ... no problem at all, sir..."

They each sipped their drinks, silently weighing their innermost thoughts for verbal exposure.

"I suppose you're wondering why I called you here, " Smith, Sr. offered somberly.

"Actually -- well, yes sir. I was unfortunately not apprised of the agenda by your secretary."

Smith Sr. interrupted abruptly with a smile. "That's because there was none." He began to laugh heartily, with Bill trying desperately to conceal his obvious confusion. "Don't look so startled. You'll find there'll be many a time when you'll call unorthodox meetings for all sorts of reasons. Why, I remember the time I called a board meeting on the thirteenth hole at the Country Club. Ended up landing one of our biggest accounts. Take my word for it -- if you follow your instinct and use good common sense, you'll never go wrong."

Bill had never seen the President in such a frivolous, personal mood before, and was unwittingly staring dumbfounded at him, at a total loss for words.

Smith, Sr. didn't appear to notice, however, and continued his monologue unhindered.

"And another thing -- steer clear of those 'big' investor types -- you know who I mean. They manage to have a proposal presented at nearly every meeting. But believe me, it'll only mean trouble. I learned that lesson when I was twenty-one. Lost everything I owned because of one of them..."

He seemed to drift off suddenly with his memories and became distractedly quiet and serene. Bill remained silent, totally mystified by this whole outburst.

"Oh, damn." Smith Sr. blurted out testily, making Bill almost jump out of his seat. "Will you listen to me go on, anyway. You'd think you had all day just to sit around and hear an old man tell stories."

Finally Bill spoke defensively. "No sir, please ... I sincerely enjoy hearing about your experiences with the company."

Smith Sr. nodded slowly in understanding and agreement, "Yes ... you would ... I suppose."

"Sir?"

He sighed heavily, then said, "Look here, if you're going to be the next President of MacDonald, may he rest in peace, and Smith, you had better start calling me 'Hamilton'. No more of this 'sir' stuff."

Bill felt his heart skip a beat as the unexpected announcement aroused a churning excitement within him. "You mean ... you've made a decision? I'm to be your successor? Not your son?"

"Wait a minute." he admonished Bill lightly. "I may be a genius, but I can't possibly answer so many questions at once."

"I'm sorry, sir ... I mean Hamilton .... but this was so sudden."

"Sudden? You call six months of procrastination sudden?"

They laughed together hard and long, erasing all of their previous doubts and misgivings about each other and their futures.

"This calls for a toast." Smith Sr. said as he rang for his secretary and requested some more cognac. As he held up his glass to Bill's, he said sincerely, "Here's to the new President -- may your new position merge with the rest of your life to fulfill the everlasting happiness that you truly deserve."

The lump in Bill's throat almost restricted the fine vintage liqueur from passing by as the words rang over and over through his mind.

"Thank you -- thank you very much -- for everything." They shook hands meaningfully, as Bill stood, preparing to leave.

"Just one more thing before you go..."

Bill turned around expectantly, and Smith Sr. wearily leaned back in his recliner, gazing out over his prized blossoms. "Don't work too hard ... please."

CHAPTER EIGHT

Jenny was back on all her normal rounds now, and therefore usually only had time to stop and see Bernie for a few minutes each day. He had progressed rapidly and was eating normally, and even walking around more and more each day.

She rounded the corner and nearly knocked him over with her forceful stride.

"Hey. What are you trying to do? Break my leg or something so you can come sit by my bedside again?" Bernie teased playfully.

She winked and smiled seductively, entwining her arm in his as she steadied him on his journey down the hallway. "Why, doctor, what a promiscuous thing to suggest." She snuggled closer to his ear. "But not a bad idea at that. Then we could spend the wee hours of the night together..."

"Tsk, tsk. You'd think a person in your profession would have more respect for a man in my condition."

She took the challenge delightedly, "Believe me, Dr. White, I'll never lose respect for your 'condition'."

They turned and proceeded back towards his room, laughing together wickedly and enjoying the questioning looks they received from the other nurses and interns on the floor.

She helped him back into bed and covered him with tender loving care, replacing her frivolous attitude with one of sincere concern.

"So tell me truthfully, now, how are you feeling today?"

"Sweetheart, I feel stronger and healthier every time I see you. I'd almost swear those two weeks in that arctic climate have increased my healing capabilities." He smiled and added, "Just think, maybe you're involved with a super-human man..."

"You mean you just found that out?" Jenny asked, pretending surprise. "You honestly don't think I'd ever settle for anything less, do you?"

They both laughed and he answered thoughtfully, "No ... no, I guess not, now that you mention it."

They talked easily about the other minor developments in the clinic that day, and after ten minutes Jenny looked at the clock and said, "Time for one of us to get back to work ... and I don't think you're quite up to it yet." She gave his blankets one last tug to ensure he was comfortable and safe.

"I always wanted a woman who'd be willing to be the breadwinner in the family…" he said, with a smug look of satisfaction crossing his face.

His mention of a permanent relationship took Jenny by surprise, but she camouflaged her reaction professionally, kissed him goodbye and went on about her duties for the day.

She was still thinking about Bernie a couple of hours later when she heard her name being paged over the loudspeaker. She picked up a nearby phone and announced, "Nurse Perrino," hearing the operator say, "One moment, please."

"What are ya' doin' for dinner ta'night, sweetheart?" The imitation of Cagney was obvious but very unconvincing.

Jenny responded by trying her best to sound like Mae West. "Well, I don't know, big boy, how about comin' on up to my place?"

"Naw, I heard the chow's better in room 502. See ya' at seven?"

She answered in her normal voice, "Sure, Bernie. But do me a favor and practice up on your voice imitations before I get there, okay?"

"Sure, sweetheart..." The phone clicked and she smiled as she replaced the receiver, ignoring the surrounding laughs of the nurses at the counter.

She had planned on running home for a quick shower and change before meeting Bernie for dinner, but gave up the idea when she found it was 6:30 by the time she finished her rounds. A patient had developed acute pneumonia while on a skiing vacation and she and the attending physician spent almost two hours with him before they were satisfied his condition was safely under control.

She headed for the women's lounge where she freshened her makeup and brushed back the unruly tendrils of hair from her temples. At times like this she was always thankful for her naturally wavy, long thick hair and olive complexion that needed so little attention.

Before leaving the lounge, she hung up her white uniform in her locker and glanced at her simple dark blue dress in the mirror. Satisfied with her appearance, she made her way down the hall to the elevator.

The hospital was always quieter at this hour, with most of the patients busy eating their evening meal, usually a welcome break in their confined state of being bedridden.

The door to Bernie's room was open, and she was momentarily surprised at the darkness within until her eyes adjusted and she saw the candlelit table by the window, fully adorned with white tablecloth, silvery serving dishes and a bottle of champagne chilling on the side.

Bernie sat at one side of the table, smiling broadly as he enjoyed her obvious state of suspended shock while examining his masterpiece.

"I can see you've been a busy little boy this afternoon," She said finally as she accepted the chair he offered very politely.

"Actually, I don't deserve all the credit," he admitted. "You see, Sharon ... ah, I mean Miss Greenbaum, had a lot to do with it."

"Aha! I knew it! And just how did you go about talking her into such an unorthodox arrangement?" She asked, feigning jealousy.

"Oh, it was easy. I simply offered her my body for a night of ecstasy and she couldn't possibly turn me down."

They laughed uproariously and he popped open the champagne.

"Are you sure you're allowed to drink this?" Jenny asked.

The familiar look of concern passed fleetingly over her face.

"Scout's honor." He held up the standard two fingers as he poured the bubbling liquid into their glasses.

"What shall we drink to?"

"How about your health?" she offered sincerely.

He nodded and they clinked their glasses together in the familiar tradition before sipping the delicate wine.

Bernie had ordered Saltimbocca from his favorite Italian restaurant, together with stuffed mushrooms, some delicious homemade fettucini, and zabaglione for dessert.

Jenny was truly in seventh heaven when they finished the expansive meal and were well into their second bottle of wine, a full-bodied Cabernet Sauvignon. Bernie had limited himself to drinking only two glasses, and Jenny found herself beginning to feel the effects of drinking the remainder.

As they sat relaxing in the stillness of the sleeping hospital, her thoughts began to drift easily. She found herself thinking once again about her dreams of Bernie and wondering at their meaning.

As if reading her mind, Bernie asked softly, "Having pleasant dreams?"

She looked into his soft, loving eyes for a moment before answering.

"As a matter of fact, I was just thinking about some dreams I've been having lately." She took another sip of wine and continued, slowly, unsure what Bernie would say. "I can't quite figure them out."

"I hope you're dreaming of me and not someone else, at least." he teased lightly, taking her hand gently in his.

She answered seriously, regaining his serious attention, "Yes, you were very much a part of these dreams."

"Tell me about them." He prodded gently.

She shifted in her chair and sat back comfortably, remembering. "Well, I always seem to be in some strange place ... a place with no real description actually...and there's a lot of people there, sort of surrounding me in a funny, unrealistic way. Almost as if they were really all *around* me." She hesitated momentarily for a reaction from Bernie. He simply nodded, indicating for her to go on. "I mean not just in front of or beside me, but sort of up above, below, and, well ... totally enveloping me in a warm, wonderful way..." She shook her head in dismay at not being able to put this part of the dream into appropriate words, and then continued.

"Anyway, I couldn't say who any of these people are, and yet I always feel I know them all very well ... almost as if ... well, as if they were somehow a part of me..." This was the first time she had ever come close to any type of meaningful analysis of her own dreams and she surprised herself in her new observation.

She accepted another glass of wine and took a sip before going on. Bernie waited patiently, while his own mind raced with inexplicable correlations between Jenny's dreams and something he felt inside but couldn't quite pinpoint.

"Suddenly -- I don't know how or why -- I then seem to find myself in a room ... with a fireplace ... and ... lots of books..." She closed her eyes and tried to picture the room clearly, not noticing Bernie's involuntary flinch at her description of what seemed to be his own den at home, and a fleeting reminder of something he too had experienced.

"There's a big desk at one end, and two big sofas facing each other in front of the fireplace." She opened her eyes suddenly, "You know, it's a lot like your den, now that I think about it. In fact, maybe that's where that idea came from."

"Could be," Bernie tried to keep his voice steady. "Do you remember anything more about your dream?"

"Yes ... this is where you come in ... but..." She stopped, grimacing as she tried once again to explain her dream sequence to herself.

"But?"

"Well, this is the part I really can't figure out. You're there with me, but you don't know me -- as me…"

"I beg your pardon?"

"Oh, I know it's confusing, but we always seem to carry on a lengthy discussion -- in this room ... your den I guess – and the whole time I know who you are but you don't know me as me, 'Jenny'. And to top it off, it doesn't seem to matter to me in my dream, but only when I wake up. It's all so strange..."

They both remained thoughtfully quiet for several moments. Jenny was still trying to decipher any hidden meaning in her recurring dreams, and Bernie found himself reaching for and trying to grasp the pieces of an inner framework that tormentingly kept flashing past his conscious mind. He wasn't sure if these were parts of dreams he himself had had, or possibly some other completely unknown tie with Jenny's recital of her dreams.

Finally, he offered, "I don't know why, but for some reason the whole time you were telling me about your dreams, I felt somehow connected or ... related -- almost like what they call 'deja-vu.' I can't really explain it, but maybe I've been having similar dreams and just can't remember them..."

She nodded and again they remained silent as a few more moments passed by. Jenny took another sip of her wine and decided to tell him the rest of her strange experience. "There was one other dream -- or what seemed to be a dream -- that I had before you were ... well ... revived."

Bernie looked up, listening intently again.

"I was at home asleep, and I dreamt you were there with me -in my bed. You reached out to touch my face and I told you out loud that I loved you, at the same time realizing you couldn't be there because you were ... well, you know. Anyway, you -- or your apparition -- disappeared, but I've always felt absolutely sure that some part of you was there with me..." She leaned over to put her head on his shoulder. "The feeling of love was so strong..."

Bernie barely heard her last words or noticed her soft cheek pressing closely against his shoulder. For what seemed to be a long passage of time, but he knew to be only a moment, he saw the whole experience clearly in his mind. It was almost as if a motion picture clip was being rerun for his benefit.

He saw and felt himself lying next to Jenny, reaching out for her just as she had said. He felt the love flow freely between them as she murmured the words, "I love you." Then in the flick of an instant, as he saw her becoming totally awake, he felt a sense of dissipation, as if he didn't have the strength to stay there with her and then suddenly, he saw he was in his den, and sitting across from him was a woman. She seemed so very familiar ...

"Honey? Are you okay?" At the sound of her voice, he blinked and saw Jenny was drying tears from her eyes.

"You're crying ... why sweetheart?" he asked gently, regaining his sense of surroundings.

"I don't know..."

He stood and took her in his arms, rocking her back and forth soothingly until her tender sobs stopped and she raised her lips to his for a lingering, loving kiss.

"I love you so much, Bernie."

"And I love you, little one."

They kissed again more passionately now, releasing all of their pent-up hunger for each other over the past months and forgetting temporarily the inner confusion they had just experienced.

Bernie's hand roamed freely over her soft, supple body and she responded quickly, untying his bathrobe and reaching inside to caress him gently. He groaned with ecstasy, as an uncontrollable climax overcame him.

"Sorry about that, love -- but it's been a long time -- too long." He reached behind her and unzipped her dress, guiding it swiftly off her shoulders and letting it fall to the floor. Jenny glanced at the closed door to the corridor and he assured her, "Don't worry, we won't be disturbed. That was the other thing I made sure of."

They made love slowly, tenderly, exploring again all the familiar hills and valleys of their bodies as they molded into one. Bernie was entirely spent after their brief but beautiful reunion, and he fell swiftly into a relaxed sleep with Jenny nestled cozily in his embrace.

"You really shouldn't tax your physical body like that, you know." Electra scolded good-naturedly.

Bernie walked over to the bookcase behind the desk, ignoring her intended jibe.

"After all, we can't be responsible for 'undue stress and misuse' of our physical bodies." She continued, teasingly.

He picked a book at random and began flipping through the pages at random.

"I'll take the risk," he smiled mischievously, *"Besides, I have a feeling you're just as guilty as I am..."*

He dropped the book on the desk and stared at her pointedly.

Electra changed into the old man form before answering, "And just what is that supposed to mean?"

"It won't do you any good to change your appearance .... 'Jenny'", he stated flatly.

She returned to her womanly state. "Well! I'm impressed!" She stood and stretched leisurely before continuing, "You really are learning quite fast. Would you care to elaborate?"

"Certainly." Bernie circled the desk to stand beside her.

"I had done some research on the gestalt theory before my 'temporary death', where it follows that each of us has some sort of 'oversoul.' This oversoul is in fact a manifestation of a group of us under its realm of being. Each of us in the group, in turn, retains certain traits, if you will, from our gestalt when in our physical state. This, in fact, establishes a direct relationship with each other and our gestalt, which is why I felt I knew you." He hesitated for a moment. "Jenny, in her physical state in my earth realm, is part of your gestalt – just as you are her oversoul."

Electra nodded, apparently waiting for him to continue.

"My only question is, then, if what I've said is true, then why are you teaching me too, unless perhaps I am related also or a part of the same gestalt?"

Electra smiled and began to explain slowly. "You have lived many lives and have learned, although you do not remember, that there are those who are called 'teachers,' for lack of a better word, who are in advanced states of being. That is not to say they know all, for no 'individual' can learn total universal knowledge, since it exists only on the highest level where we all become one, and one with the universe."

She paused, then continued, her form fading and clearing as she momentarily shifted her point of concentration. "You are correct, more or less, in your understanding of my relationship with Jenny. What you cannot know, however, is that she is in a lower learning level than you are when out of your physical state."

She paused momentarily, giving Bernie a much desired respite in which to try to digest what she was saying.

"Now, to answer your question about my 'teaching' you, I must confess that I am indeed more of a 'student' than you are."

Bernie began to question this statement, but she held up her hand, indicating silence.

"Under these unusual circumstances, you cannot delve into your bank of universal information as I can, and therefore, unfortunately, you cannot comprehend or appreciate the advanced state of knowledge you possess when you are between your physical existences."

She paused again. "What I am trying to say, most simply, is that in this realm, you are the 'teacher', not I."

Bernie interrupted. "Now I really don't understand the correlation between you and I in these meetings..."

Electra settled down once more on the sofa, at the same time inducing the fire to again spread it's glow warmly around the room. "As you already pointed out, your Jenny has a most distinct connection with my energy force. It is for this reason that you chose me prior to the initiation of this experience to more or less 'rendezvous' with during this part of your transition." She smiled serenely as he thought over the evening's discussions.

"If I'm a 'teacher,'" he mused, "then I must have access to the...'Speakers'..." He was rapidly remembering all the various data he had read on the entire life after death theory. Specifically, he now recalled the highest form of 'teacher,' at that point called a "Speaker." These Speakers had presumably successfully scaled the dimensional ladder and were nearing the very apex.

As if on cue, the room dissolved into nothingness and in it's place an assemblage of entities rapidly began taking form.

Bernie felt an overwhelming warmth enveloping his entire body.

"Good morning, darling."

He opened his eyes and found Jenny pressed extremely close to him, her arms and legs entwined with his.

"Hello, my love." He kissed the top of her head lovingly and stroked her bare shoulder. "I was having a strange, but pleasant dream..."

Jenny jerked her head up suddenly and said, "Really? So was I. What was yours about?"

Frowning slightly as he tried to clearly remember, Bernie began, "Well, I'm pretty sure I was in my den again ... and I wasn't alone, I know. But that part is fuzzy. Anyway, just before waking up, I was in some type of fantastic place filled with love and light -- but nothing concrete -- it's really hard to describe."

"Not really," answered Jenny as she smiled mischievously. "I think I know <u>exactly</u> what you're talking about." She giggled, then rapidly sobered as she noticed Bernie's serious face. She snuggled closer and went on. "My dream was a lot like yours..."

She stopped and looked up into his eyes. "As a matter of fact, I'd go so far as to say EXACTLY like yours…"

Just as the impact of her words hit them both, their attention shifted as they heard the early morning noises in the hallway indicating a new shift of nurses was coming on duty.

"I have to go." Jenny sat up suddenly, giving him a kiss before hopping out of bed and heading for the bathroom. "I can hear the rumors all over the hospital already: 'Nurse Perrino gives intensive care to heart transplant patient'."

"Just don't make a practice of it with other post-op patients." he teased as she shut the door behind her.

Bernie's dream was still fresh in his mind and he took out a pad and pencil and recorded in detail all that he could remember. At the same time, he decided to have a chat with Gerry -- perhaps he could shed some light on his and Jenny's experiences.

Dick and Theresa took the early flight to Chicago and arrived promptly at 10:00 in the morning.

Dick had explained to Theresa his connection with Bernie, but she still failed to recognize the name as being the same as the man she had met long ago on a plane flight. Dick didn't go into the feelings that had been stirred up upon his reading of the news of his friend's accomplishment. Somehow, he knew his life, and hopefully Theresa's as well, was about to change. He only hoped it would be for the better, but was willing to accept whatever might happen without remorse. The one important thing he had reaffirmed from reading about Bernie's experience, even before talking to him, was that life is only a passing existence -- and it's not how much money you make that matters -- it's what you do with your life that counts.

Theresa had sat quietly listening to her husband on the plane as he spoke of this Dr. White he had known only briefly. She was silently amazed at how Dick had changed since hearing the news of this doctor's death and "resurrection". Without realizing it, she felt strangely attracted to the idea of meeting this person, and had been easily persuaded to change her plans and leave a day early. She was also aware of the new sense of pride she felt for her husband -- almost as if she enjoyed being dominated -- for a change.

Upon arriving in Chicago, they took a cab to the clinic and were inching their way through crowded traffic when Dick asked the driver, "Is it always like this? I feel right at home on these freeways -- just like L. A."

Harry forced a half-hearted smile and answered over his shoulder, "Yeah." He glanced at the attractive, well-dressed black couple in the back seat and found himself wondering how they got their bucks – seemed like everybody but Harry could do well for themselves.

Dick settled back after seeing that the cab driver was no friendlier than those in L. A. Finally, they pulled up in front of the clinic. Dick had planned on asking about a hotel nearby, but decided to ask inside instead.

Harry watched them walk up the steps to the building and his thoughts drifted to his one friend in the world, Bernie. He had wanted to stop so many times to see him, but he couldn't seem to find the courage. After all, what would he say? Maybe Bernie wouldn't even remember him after being through such an experience.

He shook his head and pulled into the traffic, spotting a rider up ahead on the sidewalk waving his arms frantically to signal the cab to pull over.

"Dr. Bernard White's room, please," Dick requested of the graying, unsmiling nurse at the front desk.

"I'm sorry, sir, but Dr. White is not allowed to have visitors."

She turned to go back to her filing.

"But, excuse me, ma'am. We've flown all the way from Los Angeles to see him. You see, Dr. White and I worked together on the plans for a new wing at..."

"I'm sorry," she interrupted testily, "but, as I said, no visitors."

Jenny was walking through the lobby and couldn't help but overhear the conversation between the young black couple and old Mrs. Stapleton. She walked rapidly over to Dick's side to intercede.

"Excuse me, did you say you flew in from L. A. to see Dr. White?"

Dick and Theresa turned in surprise to face the pretty young nurse.

"Uh, yes, that's right." Theresa offered timidly.

Mrs. Stapleton was about to interrupt again when Jenny said, "Excuse us, please. Would you come with me? Perhaps I can be of assistance."

Dick smiled devilishly over his shoulder at the receptionist, who was obviously upset at being overridden.

Jenny walked them into the lounge area and they all sat down while Dick briefly outlined his acquaintance with Bernie.

"And you came all this way just to see him?" Jenny asked a little skeptically.

"Well, not exactly, Miss...uh..." Theresa hesitated.

"Perrino -- but you can call me Jenny, since you're friends of Bernie's." She winked and smiled broadly.

"Thanks, Jenny. Anyway, as I was saying, I was..." Theresa glanced at her smiling husband, "I mean 'we' were on our way to New York and decided to leave a day early and stop off here in Chicago. You see, my husband and I feel somewhat compelled to speak to Dr. White about his experience. I can't really explain why, but I assure you we won't take much of his time. Unless, of course, as his nurse you don't feel he's up to it..."

Jenny couldn't help laughing, as she answered, "Oh, he's up to it, alright. And I'm not his nurse by the way -- just a very *close* friend, if you know what I mean." She winked again and they all laughed together.

Jenny stood up and glanced at her watch. "Well, it's almost lunchtime, so he should hopefully be in his room. Let me show you the way."

Dick hesitated momentarily, "Are you sure it's okay? We can always come back another time."

"He might be out for tests this afternoon, and I really think right now is a better time to see him," Jenny assured them. She turned and walked towards the elevator with Dick and Theresa following closely behind.

As they walked into Bernie's room, Jenny announced playfully, "You know you're getting popular when people come all the way from the West Coast to see you."

Bernie looked up in surprise to see Dick enter the room behind Jenny. His eyes really widened when he recognized Theresa at Dick's side. As everyone else thought, he too saw that they made a perfect couple.

"Dick --what a surprise!" Bernie extended his hand to shake Dick's.

"Dr. White ... I mean Bernie -- it's great to see you too. This is my wife, Theresa..." he moved aside to let her step closer so she could also shake his hand. Bernie glanced over to see a smiling Jenny standing in the doorway, then looked directly into Theresa's tantalizing brown eyes. A corresponding look of recognition had spread over her face, and she exclaimed happily, "Bernie! It's you!"

The quizzical looks on Dick's and Jenny's faces made both Bernie and Theresa break into uncontrollable laughter. Finally, Bernie composed himself enough to explain.

"You see, Theresa and I met on a flight out of L. A. -- right after I met with you, as a matter of fact." He nodded at Dick, then went on. "Anyway, I was perfectly delighted with your wife." At this point he winked conspiratorially towards Dick and then Jenny. "In more ways than one, I might add."

Everyone laughed at his delightful honesty, even Jenny, who reinforced her pride in the man she loved.

Theresa sat down on a nearby chair and admitted, "I can't believe you're the same person either. I have memories of a conservative white dude sitting next to me on this airplane, going out of his way to be friendly with me…" She looked over at Jenny and smiled. "I thought he was a dirty old man, until I got to know him better."

"I'm in luck," Bernie chimed in happily. "I actually fooled another one."

Everyone laughed at his friendly humor, and in the meantime, Dick and Theresa settled down in some chairs opposite Bernie's bed. He was obviously feeling very well after his experience, and began inconspicuously doing some mild isometric exercises as he sat on the side of his bed.

"So, what really brings you two to Chicago?" Bernie asked, as he flexed his strengthening leg muscles.

Dick glanced at Theresa, then answered for them both. "We wanted to see you -- and, to be perfectly truthful, after what you've been through, we both felt we needed to talk to you."

Bernie smiled in his overwhelmingly comforting way, glanced at Jenny, then said, "I hate to disappoint you, but there's not much more to say about the whole ordeal than what has already been published by the press."

A silence hung in the air as Dick and Theresa tried to search for the right words to say. Theresa was the first to speak.

"I can't help but wonder -- as I guess the whole world does -- just how it feels to be ... well ... "

"Dead?" Bernie supplied the word for her.

Theresa felt the blood rise to her cheeks and found herself staring at the floor to avoid any further embarrassment. Bernie walked over to where they were sitting and pulled up another chair to face them directly.

He began slowly. "You see, there wasn't anything specific in the papers about my death experience simply because I really don't remember much." He stopped, rubbing his chin thoughtfully. "I do, however, know for sure that the soul ... spirit ... or whatever you want to call it -- does survive after physical death."

His statement was so firm that Dick and Theresa silently looked at him, apprehension and confusion showing clearly in their eyes.

Bernie looked at Jenny, who was listening quietly at one side, and wondered if Gerry had told her about his immediate experiences after death. He decided to continue, since he wanted Jenny to know the story in any event.

"I don't know how much, if any, you two know about death experiences in general -- where the person is revived in some manner." He paused and noted the blank looks on their faces before continuing. "Well, you see, there are thousands of fully documented cases where people recall their experiences after being pronounced clinically dead. They all seem to fall into the same general sequence of events."

He stood and walked over to the window, pushing the curtains aside as he spoke.

"I'm afraid I followed the same initial steps as the others. I found myself -- whatever that 'self' is -- outside my physical body, in fact, right up there." He turned and pointed up to a corner of the room above the door. Everyone followed his gaze in awe and amazement before returning their attention to Bernie.

"Then the lights went out." He paused, and shook his head, saying, "The next thing I knew, I was coming out of a coma and looking into the homely face of one of the night nurses. Nearly scared her to death, I think -- no pun intended."

He laughed loudly before noticing the somber looks on everyone else's faces. "Oh, come on now. You all act like death and dying are terrible, frightening subjects. I hoped the world would think a little differently after witnessing my fine specimen of a body survive the 'grasp of death' and 'live' to tell about it."

His try at lightening the tone of the conversation seemed to be failing miserably, until Jenny interceded. "I can vouch for one aspect of his new 'life'…" She nudged Dick playfully, encouraging a smile out of both he and Theresa.

Bernie scowled at Jenny for her statement momentarily, until she added, "It's okay love, I told them we were 'good friends'."

At that, the tense atmosphere seemed to fade noticeably as everyone relaxed and settled back comfortably in their chairs.

Dick was the next to speak as he asked, "If there's really some type of existence after our body dies, as you suggest, then it would seem that we ... I mean ... the people on earth in general, don't know a heck of a lot about the 'meaning' of it all." He stopped to think a moment. "I mean,   I'm not a religious person,   but my parents always preached to us kids about being God-fearing children or else we'd go to Hell and all that.   No one ever mentioned any real 'life' after death. It was always 'be good and you'll go to heaven.' Be bad, and you know what – the Devil himself will come to get you." He laughed at his remembrance of his early childhood.

Theresa broke in to add, "Yeah, it was the same with me, but we were convinced to be good by a picture of angels with harps, wings and halos to boot."

Bernie looked into Jenny's eyes to see, much to his delight, the same recognition of feeling on the subject -- most probably as a result of their dual experiences,

Bernie regained Dick and Theresa's attention as he reached over and grasped each of their hands in his. The room again filled with silent expectance before he said, "I believe it's good that you both remember and identify with your early religious training. There is much that is exaggerated -- much that is neglected -- but basically all religion serves a much needed purpose in our society, regardless of which faith you believe in."

Bernie sighed heavily. "It's all fairly simple, really. I believe you're confined to a physical body to learn the valuable and pertinent lessons necessary to further your development. You see, I think we achieve this 'development' by returning to a physical state, as we know it, many times -- as many times as is necessary to 'learn our lessons' satisfactorily. Some people call it 'reincarnation', but for some reason that word doesn't quite fit my understanding. I guess because of the misconceptions people have tied to the word over the years.

"In any case, your lives are really nothing more than a 'test' of what you've learned in previous lives. If you pass the tests, you progress, if not..." he shrugged his shoulders meaningfully, you must come back and try, try again."

Dick and Theresa were thoroughly mind-boggled by the abrupt, incongruous lecture Bernie had given to them, and sat quietly stunned, trying to evaluate his words.

Jenny, however, found -- much to her amazement -- that she not only understood what Bernie had said, but had anticipated his thoughts even before they were verbalized.

Across the room, Bernie realized he felt very strange, as if his physical body was weighted down and a dull heaviness had enveloped him, with his conscious mind struggling to regain complete awareness.

Gradually, he felt more like himself and tried to remember clearly the last words he had spoken. "I'm sorry, I didn't mean to ramble on so..."

"No, please ... don't apologize." Dick admonished. "I can't explain it, but somehow your observations have made me realize what life -- this life anyway -- is all about. I've been so confused about things..." he glanced at Theresa and saw silent understanding in her beautiful brown eyes.

"I think we should all stop getting so overly involved with our petty problems and disappointment in day-to-day life, and concentrate solely on our ultimate goals. And I now know that helping others to realize this belief will be my first step toward accomplishing those goals."

Theresa found herself feeling rather lighthearted. It was clear to her that she had thought only of herself all these years. She sadly admitted that her goals had always been self-centered. Never once had she considered those around her as any part whatsoever of her 'lifetime.'

As she felt a dreary state of depression rapidly approaching her, she shook her head and stood up to announce:

"Your simple explanation has opened up my narrow outlook on life -- what do they call it, 'tunnel vision?'" She hurried on to avoid the questioning stares of everyone around her. As she spoke, she walked over to the window to gaze out, pensively.

"Why is it we always seem to realize things like this so <u>late</u> in life? It could have been so different..."

"It's never too late," Jenny inserted comfortingly.

Theresa turned to face everyone once again. Fleetingly, she thought to herself, "It may not be too late to recognize where I went wrong, but can we expect to erase the damage we've already done to our marriage?" Somehow she already knew the answer.

Aloud, she went on, "Anyway, regardless of everything else, we need to concentrate on the future." She smiled broadly and everyone murmured their agreement.

Dick held Theresa's gaze for just a moment, then stood up and took her hand. "Shall we leave Bernie alone so he can finish his rejuvenation without further interruptions?"

Bernie walked over to join them and added playfully, "Well, I wouldn't go quite that far." He put his arm around Jenny's slim waist and pulled her close to him, smiling meaningfully. "Jenny is the reason I'm making such a fast recovery. You know -- certain 'exercises' and 'procedures' that only she can perfect."

They all laughed together and Jenny poked Bernie in the side, a slight flush of embarrassment reddening her face.

After everyone promised to keep in touch, Dick and Theresa left, saying they had decided to fly to Las Vegas for a few days, canceling any business plans they had previous had. They wanted to get away for a few days and think about their new lives.

Bernie and Jenny went over a sat side by side on the edge of his bed, holding hands like young lovers.

"Why do you suppose they picked Las Vegas?" Jenny asked after a moment.

"I don't know. Maybe that was where they got married ... and they want a second honeymoon..."

Jenny wasn't quite convinced. "I hope so..."

They were quiet for another short time, and then Jenny leaned closer to Bernie and kissed his earlobe seductively. He turned with a groan and whispered between kisses, "Hey--wanna fool around?"

Jenny giggled and jumped up to go throw the latch on the door and put out the "Do Not Disturb" sign that Gerry had thoughtfully procured for them.

Dick and Theresa arrived in Las Vegas late that evening and were promptly checked in at Caesar's Palace on the fourteenth floor.

They still had not spoken more than a few words to each other when they finally reached their room, a spacious suite; with a balcony overlooking the city and a beautifully tended courtyard directly below.

Theresa was standing by the window quietly enjoying the view of the busy city around her, when she felt a tingling sensation run down her spine as Dick.caressed her shoulders. She shivered involuntarily and turned slowly to face him. With a newfound sincerity and warmth, they embraced each other possessively.

"I'm scared..." Theresa murmured against Dick's shoulder.

"I know -- I am too." He held her for another moment, then pulled her away at arm's length and looked deep into her searching eyes. "Shall I start? Or do you want to?"

She shook her head and said, "No, you go ahead. I think we both feel the same way anyway."

He nodded and took her over to a comfortable couch to sit down, facing each other.

"Basically, I think we've both come to certain important realizations that will certainly change the rest of our lives."

She agreed, and he went on, thoughtfully.

"As far as I'm concerned, as I told Bernie, I want to re-establish my goals in life on much broader terms. This way, I won't get bogged down and side-tracked by all the petty and mundane things."

Then Theresa spoke, softly yet firmly. "I have a lot of work to do to straighten out my life also. I feel as if there's a huge void around me that never existed before, only because I never looked any further than my own selfish interests before. Now I intend to fill that void, very gradually, by giving of myself to help others -- I can already think of several ways. And you know something? It really is a wonderful new feeling. And this is only the beginning."

They were both smiling happily, individually contemplating their new feelings.

They came out of their respective revelries almost simultaneously, and Dick said, "And our marriage? I think we share the same feelings..."

She nodded and said, "Yes, I do too. Ours was always a marriage of convenience rather than the loving union it should have been." She hesitated, then went on hurriedly. "Not that I don't love you, because I do -- as a person, as a friend, even as a lover." They laughed and winked at each other knowingly.

Dick continued on for her. "Yeah, I'll always love you too, babe. But as 'friends' we'll be much happier in our individual lives, right?"

"Right. Who knows? Our relationship will probably be a whole lot better on this basis. I'll get a cute little place over in Westwood, and have you over for dinner and dancing -- and whatever else might happen." She giggled playfully and threw her arms around Dick happily.

Somehow they both felt totally relieved and completely at ease with their new arrangement.

"Do you want a divorce now, or wait until morning, Mrs. Pearson?" Dick teased formally.

"Well...I'd like to do just one more thing as your legal married wife..."

Theresa felt her head spinning with a delightful release, since she had rediscovered herself and her true feelings toward the man she had been married to for so long. She let herself float in the strength of his arms as he carried her slowly to the large, ornately decorated king-size bed.

The sounds of the city outside seemed to melt away as they gave of each other in a fresh and beautifully enlightening way. No longer did they make love in the calculated, mechanical way of the past, with only their bodily satisfaction in mind. Now, as never before, their innermost selves flowed ecstatically forth, giving each other a feeling of such rejuvenation they never dreamed possible. Time and time again they flew to the top of the highest mountains together, then leaped into the clouds with rejoice at their newly acquired oneness.

Finally, physically spent and at peace with themselves and the world around them, they drifted into a soft valley of slumber together.

Bill lowered his head to smell the sweet fragrance of the gardenia corsage he was holding as he rang the doorbell of Anne's apartment. She opened the door with a sweeping, sensual movement all her own and raised up on her toes to kiss him hello.

Bill stood back slightly to gaze on her beautiful appearance. "You look absolutely gorgeous,"

"Why, thank you." She twirled playfully before him, accepting the corsage as he entered the room. "I'm glad you like it."

Her delicate gown flowed symmetrically about her as he admired her from arms-length. The bodice was cut enticingly low, revealing the soft, white mounds of her breasts, and Bill found himself staring helplessly in that general direction.

Pleased with her purposefully distractive tactics, Anne guided him over to her built-in bar where they sat comfortably on a pair of barstools.

"The usual?"

"Allow me." He proceeded to pour their drinks with expertise, then offered a toast. "To the new President of MacDonald and Smith."

Anne nearly dropped her glass at his words. "Wha ... what did you say? You don't mean..."

Bill nodded, smiling broadly. He barely had time to set his glass down before she flew into his arms, hugging him wildly.

"Oh, Bill. This is so wonderful! I just knew you'd get the appointment."

She planted a great big kiss on his cheek, then stood back, holding his hand affectionately. "So tell me all about it -- when, where, and how. And don't you dare leave out a single detail."

Bill laughed at her happy excitement, and proceeded to describe his unusual meeting with Smith Sr. that afternoon.

"When is the big day you take over and promote me to Senior VP?" she asked seductively.

"Unofficially, I start right away. Officially, at the Board meeting scheduled for next week. And don't laugh about your promotion ... after all, I could be 'persuaded'..." he hinted impishly.

"Oh, you ... you male chauvinist! See what we women have to do to climb the professional ladder..." She paused then added, "In this case, I love it. Don't tell the ERA people, though."

She nuzzled up close to him, saving his strength and feeling secure by his side. He put his arm around her protectively, and admitted, "Don't tell any of my male associates, but I couldn't have made it without you,

Annie. I only hope I can be the man you want me to be..." he whispered softly.

"You can ... and you will be. Just take old Smith's advice, following your natural instinct, and, most importantly, don't work too hard."

They looked into each other's eyes tenderly for a moment, then Bill announced, "This calls for a celebration. Where shall we go tonight?"

Anne took another sip of her drink, cautiously studying the man across from her over the rim of her glass.

"Well, if you're in an adventurous mood..." she began casually.

"Aren't I always?" Bill answered playfully.

They laughed and she said, "Okay, then, I was told that the dinner show at the Timbers is really interesting -- and the food is supposed to be delicious."

"Sounds great." Bill agreed easily as they finished their drinks and headed for the door.

Neither of them had ever been to the Timbers before, but Anne had heard it was a great place to go. As they entered the restaurant, it took them bath a few moments to adjust to the dimness before discerning the handsome maitre'd approaching them, smiling broadly,

They were shown to a nice corner table bordering the stage in the center of the room. Bill shifted in his seat to eye the stage skeptically. "What type of show is it?"

Anne winked and answered truthfully, "Well, I heard that it's a very different type of performance..."

"Oh, really?"

"It's not anything like that," she reprimanded him sharply. "In fact, I'm surprised you would think I would want to see 'that' type of show." She blushed, then added, "whatever 'that' type of show is -- I wouldn't know, I've never seen one..." She was obviously embarrassed at her own naivete and turned away as the waiter poured their water.

"I'm sorry, honey. I didn't mean to embarrass you." He grasped her hand tightly and she looked into his eyes forgivingly,

"It's okay ... honest." She picked up the menu and scanned the contents quickly. "Let's order -- I'm starving."

Their dinner was delightful and each of them felt a wonderful sense of fulfillment, both bodily and mentally, as they sipped their Irish coffee at the end of the meal.

They were talking of some recent funny happenings at the office when the lights lit up the stage and the small three-piece band began to play some introduction music. An unseen voice announced, "And now, ladies and gentlemen, we proudly present the MC of our show, Mr. Guy Nelson."

There was a dramatic drum roll and a short, stocky, curly-haired MC stepped out to greet the audience, pleased at the reception he received.

"Why, thank you, thank you, thank you." he said as he waved his arms meaningfully toward the crowd.

He told a few old, corny jokes which everyone enjoyed nevertheless. Anne and Bill shook their heads, surprised at their own laughter at the silly puns and one-liners.

After about ten minutes of this monologue, the MC nodded at the band, signaling another drum roll, and announced: "And now, the moment you've all been waiting for. The highlight of our show, other than me of course..." he paused for the anticipated laughter, "Miss Gayle Starr."

He stepped aside as an attractive blond woman in her mid-thirties walked to center stage, smiling and bowing slightly to the audience until the roar of applause died down.

"Good evening. You all look wonderful tonight." Her voice was as smooth as silk, and Bill waited for her to break into a song at any moment.

"May I ask how many of you have been here before?" Quite a few people raised their hands, and she added, "Great. It always helps to reassure our newcomers when they see that people really do enjoy this crazy show." She paused as the expected buzz of acknowledgment and laughter passed through the crowd.

"For those of you not familiar with my particular talent, I'd like to explain beforehand that what you will see and perhaps experience is totally realistic. There are no tricks involved whatsoever, or believe me, the government would never let me continue."

Bill marveled again at the strange quality of her voice and her magnetic personality. He couldn't help but feel entranced by this unusual person.

She continued, stepping off the stage to wander amongst the tables, the spotlight following her every move.

"You see, my 'talent' is commonly referred to as being a 'psychic', and my show consists simply of passing on any communications which come to me as I hold your hand."

To demonstrate, she grasped the outstretched hand of a willing woman guest, closed her eyes for a moment and then spoke. "You are concerned about your job ... you have been thinking of asking for a raise, but hesitate for fear of losing your position altogether. I see an older man with graying hair ... his name is Ben..." She looked down at the woman's startled face. "That was your father, correct?" The woman nodded excitedly and Miss Starr went on. "He says not to worry about your job -- go ahead and ask for the raise, for you are a valued worker and could not easily be replaced. He sends his love very strongly ... I feel he has not been in the spirit world very long...'" Again she looked towards the woman, who answered softly, "That's right -- he's only been gone a little over six months." She brushed an emotional tear from her eye.

"He wants you to know he is always near you and does not want you to grieve his passing anymore, for he is extremely happy and at peace now."

The audience clapped approvingly for several minutes before Miss Starr went on. Next, she approached an older lady and spoke to her about her retirement and travel plans, referring to a spirit named Lou, who was her older brother. Again, her messages were all extremely pertinent and the audience grew even more receptive to this amazing woman's abilities.

Bill and Anne were as spellbound as everyone else. As Miss Starr approached him, however, he shifted uncomfortably in his seat, averting his eyes in order to miss her penetrating gaze.

"And you, sir, I feel you are skeptical of the powers emanating from the spirit world, is that correct?" She placed her hand lightly on his shoulder.

"Well ... it's not that, actually..." he stammered.

"Wait," she interrupted. "Normally I do not give readings to anyone doubting my credibility, but I have a very strong vibration from the spirit world."

Bill again fell under her spell, allowing her to continue without a word. "Does the name Nancy mean anything to you?" Bill glanced quickly at Anne, who nodded in encouragement, before he replied, "Yes ... she was my wife..." As before, everyone in the room became extremely quiet in anticipation of her reading.

"There was something very tragic about her death ... I'm having a little difficulty receiving this ... Oh, I see ... your wife took her own life, is that correct?" The audience made a law gasping sound, unnoticed by Bill, who was hanging on her every word.

"Yes ... that's right..."

"That is why it is difficult for her to transmit her thoughts to me ... she has not yet reached the universal spirit realm as a result of her folly ... she asks for your help..."

Bill was about to speak, when she went on abruptly. "You must realize she alone was responsible for her act of self-centered desperation. Now, in order for her to cross into the universal realm, you must release her from the feelings of quilt you harbor from her passing. She tells me she has learned many important lessons after misusing the gift of her past life, and would profit immensely from your future happiness..."

She paused momentarily and then opened her eyes and spoke seriously to Bill.

"That is all. I feel this was a very important message, and hope you will take it very seriously, as I know from all *my* experience that it is not often a spirit asks for help. Usually, it is they who offer assistance to us here on earth."

Then she raised her face to the spotlight and smiled captivatingly as she went on to the next guest reading.

Anne and Bill sat in silence through the rest of the show, both of them going over and over the words she had passed on, presumably from Nancy.

After driving Anne home, Bill stopped at her front door and asked, "Mind if I come in for a while? I could use a nightcap."

"I was hoping you would." Anne replied truthfully.

She took off her coat and hung it in the hall closet as he poured some Drambuie into a pair of glasses at the bar. They sat down comfortably on the couch, and Anne nestled her head against his shoulder, tucking her feet under her.

"So, what do you think?" he asked finally.

Anne waited a moment before answering, thoughtfully picking out the right words before speaking. "If you mean do I think that was really a message from Nancy, my answer is -- 'yes'. That lady was too right-on with everyone else in the room to think otherwise. And you?"

"I'm not sure ... it isn't every day you receive a message from the dead, you know." He replied with such vehemence that she feared further comment on her part would be useless. The subject was dropped and they finished their drinks in silence.

Finally, Bill sighed and stood, then walked to the door with Anne following closely behind him. He turned and took her in his arms, kissing her soft, willing lips lovingly. Anne felt the welcome warmth spread over her entire body as she clung to him, wishing so desperately he would never leave, yet knowing that was not possible ... not yet.

"Goodnight, and thanks for being as wonderful and understanding as you are." He turned and walked down the hallway and was almost out of sight before Anne whispered, "Goodnight, my darling..."

Bill arrived early Monday morning at the office, heading immediately to the coffee machine to brew the day's first batch. He had slept fitfully both nights before, and felt slightly drugged from lack of rest. He drank thirstily from the steaming cut of liquid, anticipating the surge of awareness that always followed.

He sifted quickly through the 'in box' on his desk, matters he had neglected on Friday. He jotted down some notes as he set his priorities for the day.

By the time his secretary arrived at 8:00 a.m., he had poured over an incredible amount of work, and, after his third cup of coffee, felt satisfied with his progress so early in the day. He dictated a series of letters to her and coordinated a list of his remaining appointments for the day. Notice of his promotion to President had spread through the company like wildfire, initiating all kinds of congratulatory calls and meetings. Smith, Jr. was vacationing in Rome and would no doubt be the last to hear the news.

Before he knew it, it was 3:15 in the afternoon. He glanced at his notebook and noticing a 3:30 engagement, he sat down and quickly dialed Anne's extension.

After clearing her secretary, Bill asked Anne, "Hi -- how's your day going?"

She sighed heavily, and said, "Great ... just great. Today has been one of those days when everything goes just the opposite of how it's supposed to."

"Wait a minute." He teased lightly. "I have to get my violin out…"

"Oh, you!" She laughed along with him, and felt some of the tension floating away.

Bill went on, "Seriously, though, I was really calling to see if you had any plans for this evening -- other than visiting mysterious psychics, that is."

They laughed together again before Anne suggested, "How about a quiet dinner at my place tonight, 'Mr. President'? I bought two big juicy steaks from my favorite butcher on my lunch hour today."

"Your 'favorite' butcher, eh?" Bill teased. "Care to elaborate?"

"Sure, don't you know what it takes to get a decent cut of meat these days?" she insinuated lightly.

They giggled at each other's antics again and Bill answered, "Well, I guess I can accept your invitation, as long as _he_ won't mind."

"He?" Anne asked, confused.

"Your butcher, of course."

The rest of the day flew by swiftly, and when Bill looked at his watch it was already almost six o'clock. He would have to leave soon to make it home for a quick shower before going over to Anne's. He was just about to walk out the door when the phone rang. Surprised at the lateness of the call, Bill answered questioningly, "Hello? Anderson here."

"Bill? Bill Anderson? Is that you?" The voice on the other end crackled through the long distance wires.

"Yes ... uh ... I'm sorry, who's this?"

That unmistakable laugh rang through from the other end:

"Why, it's Bernie...Bernie White. From Chicago, remember?"

Bill sat back down at his desk, stunned at the unexpected call.

"Why yes, Dr. White. I've been thinking of you quite often lately..." he felt immediately embarrassed at his obvious meaning and stopped, then added sincerely, "I've been wondering how you were ... since ... well, since your 'operation.'"

Bernie laughed good-naturedly and replied, "Just fine, thanks. As a matter of fact, I feel better now than I did when I was in my prime. And that's been quite some time, I'll willingly admit."

"Say, that's great. Those guys you work with must really know what they're doing."

"You can say that again -- but enough about me. I'm sure you read the whole story in the papers. I'm calling to see how *you* are doing."

"Me?" Bill seemed confused.

"Yes, you. How's the blood pressure lately? I certainly hope you haven't forgotten my advice to avoid a heart attack."

"Oh, of course not. I really feel much better since we talked -- I guess I've developed some sort of attitude where things don't bother me like they used to. In fact, I was just promoted to President, and I'm not even uptight about the responsibility."

"The Presidency, eh? Sounds like a great opportunity for you ... as long as you watch your health."

Bill laughed and replied lightly, "Look who's talking about being healthy. From what you say, your 'experience' has made you feel younger already."

Bernie joined in the frivolity. "Well ... maybe I did exaggerate just a little bit."

"So tell me Bernie, what are your plans now -- a relaxing retirement?"

"Hell, no! That would <u>really</u> age me in a hurry. No, I plan to go back to being as active as possible in my practice -- as soon as my 'co-workers', as you call them, will allow me to, that is."

"Well, in that case, I'll just wait till I see you to get my next checkup, how's that sound?"

"It's a deal."

There was an awkward silence as they each waited for the other to speak. Finally, Bernie asked seriously, "Say... I was wondering ... well, I know I have no right to ask, but I thought of you often during my convalescence ... and I found myself extremely concerned about your emotional state..."

"My emotional state?" Bill echoed.

"You remember, Bill, Dr. Schottler told me about your wife's suicide and your difficulty in coping with the situation."

"Oh, yes...,"

Bernie continued rapidly, "Please believe that I don't want to interfere. After all, we've only met once and even then only briefly. It's just that for some reason ever since my 'reawakening' -- which is how I've come to refer to it -- I've felt a sort of new sense of understanding or knowledge about those in our society who take their own lives. I felt I should pass this information on to you so perhaps you can benefit from it. Do you mind?"

"No ... no, of course not -- please go on." Bill said as he felt an odd feeling of recognition flowing through him.

"Well, it's just that after experiencing death myself and the conscious feelings leading up to it, I know without a doubt that the gift of life is exactly that: a gift. It is not ours to throw away, and therefore those who do must have to suffer immensely in order to learn the enormity of their mistake. Actually, I don't feel that one 'suffers' after death in the same sense we do here in our physical state..."

Bernie hesitated, noting with interest the same strange sense of disassociation and physical heaviness that he felt when speaking to Dick and Theresa recently. He forced his conscious mind to settle back down into the background, allowing the words and thoughts to form freely from within.

"Presumably, since one no longer retains a physical body, the soul or spirit alone must traverse the unknown beyond, although I confess I'm sure it is much more capable of doing so than we like to believe.

"In any case, I seem to have learned that those who take their lives have to spend a period of time to gain this new understanding before entering the universal realm we all commonly refer to as 'Heaven'."

He paused here to make an insertion not directly related to the message he felt he had to give to Bill, but all the same realizing another phase of his new knowledge.

"You know, I've come to believe, as we speak of 'Heaven', that there is no 'Hell' -- except that which one makes for oneself by one's own doing -- whether in a physical state or not."

Bill was having a little difficulty following this conversation and was really amazed at it's content, but continued to listen intensely.

"But, getting back to the subject of suicides, the one other astounding thought that keeps coming to my mind is that the suicide souls must certainly almost always retain a tenuous tie to those they leave behind. Don't you agree?"

Bill answered unsurely, "Well, I guess so..."

"What I mean is that, in most cases, there are relatives involved who undoubtedly feel various forms of guilt or unrealistic remorse, unfairly relating themselves to the sole mistake of the suicidal individual. In other words, I guess I'm trying to say that I've somehow gained a better understanding of your feelings about your wife's death. And, strangely enough, I sincerely felt almost compelled to call you to relate my new theory."

Bernie began to feel the heaviness disappear, and again he struggled to gain a completely conscious state. At the same time, Bill felt a new realization of truth descend upon him.

"I'm really glad you called to tell me all this..." Bill said sincerely. "I guess I do have my own rather selfish reasons for keeping up a guilty facade, instead of facing the sad but realistic truth about Nancy's suicide. I want to thank you, Bernie, for once more effecting a turning point in my life."

"Well, let's not get too carried away," Bernie admonished, lapsing into his usual casual self. "After all, I just give the advice -- it's up to you to follow it."

Bill agreed heartily, "Don't worry about that. I feel like I'm already catching up with you in your new youth. Like a heavy weight has just been lifted from my shoulders. Again -- thank you. I've never met anyone who cares as much as you do about helping others -- with sincerity. I hope you'll soon feel well enough to come out to the coast to give me my physical too -- and I guarantee you'll be amazed at my new vitality."

"I promise I'll be there before you know it," Bernie replied happily. "Talk to you soon, Bill, and take care now."

"You too."

At each end of the long distance wire, the two men sat with their hands resting on their phones, smiling contentedly as they went over their enlightening conversation.

Bill arrived early for his dinner date at Anne's apartment that evening, surprised at his sudden feeling of exhilaration since talking with Bernie. Anne immediately sensed the change in him and commented lightly, as he hugged her tightly, "My, you're certainly in a good mood tonight. Any special reason?"

Bill stepped back and gave her a disdainful look. "So, it takes a 'special reason' for me to be in a good mood, eh?"

As he had intended, Anne apologized, "I'm sorry, I didn't mean it that way..."

Bill began to laugh loudly as Anne looked up at him, confused at this peculiar exchange. He whisked her into his arms once more and led her over to the balcony where the unusually clear night lay like a dark velvet background for the bright, sparkling stars sprinkled above.

Bill spoke softly in her ear as she leaned warmly against him. "I had a very important phone call earlier this evening at the office."

Immediately Anne thought it was something to do with the Presidency, and she shifted to look into his face questioningly.

"No, it's nothing to do with work, love," he assured her. "Actually, it was far more integral to my life than my job could ever be." He ignored her persistent stare of perplexity and replaced her head tenderly against his shoulder once more, stroking her soft, long hair lovingly as he explained.

"My call was from Dr. White -- the doctor who underwent cryogenic suspension to survive a later heart transplant."

Anne answered thoughtfully, "Yes, I remember the article you showed me. But what did he say that was so important?"

"Well ... " he began slowly, fitting all the pieces together to form a clear picture in his mind. "Remember the other night what that psychic woman told me about Nancy? She said I would have to help her by not feeling guilty about her suicide anymore."

"She also said Nancy wants you to be happy," Anne reminded him tenderly.

Bill kissed her lightly on the neck and went on, the wondrous new feeling of a freedom to express himself growing steadily stronger within him.

"Well, Bernie ... Dr. White, said he felt somehow 'compelled' to call me about his new understanding of suicidal personalities. And what was really amazing was the fact that he said virtually the same that the psychic said -- that I must stop feeling guilty in order to allow Nancy to progress."

He twirled her around to face him, grasping her arms tightly as he said, "Oh, honey, don't you see? I've finally freed myself. Nancy's death never was my fault."

Tears of happiness welled up uncontrollably in Anne's eyes as she found herself completely overwhelmed by Bill's realization. Suddenly, they were in each other's arms, kissing and hugging each other as if there was no tomorrow.

For the first time, they both reveled in their newfound ability to be honest, open and in love.

Laughing and behaving outrageously, they skipped dinner and gave of each other throughout the night, travelling to uncharted heights of ecstasy together.

They experimented in their lovemaking, teaching and learning freely and openly from each other.

At last, they were truly one, as deep inside, both of them realized their complete union had always been inevitable.

CHAPTER NINE

It was Sunday afternoon, and Jenny was spending the entire day with Bernie. They played cards, went for a walk, had a light lunch together and were now concentrating on a game of Monopoly. When Gerry walked in, he was hardly noticed by the high-financing pair at the table.

"So this is what you two do in private?" ' he teased good-naturedly.

"Shhh! Can't you see she's headed for Park Place? I've invested everything in that hotel, and if she'll just roll a six…" Bernie rubbed his hands greedily.

"Ten!" Jenny called out, happily bouncing her piece past 'GO' and collecting $200.00 from the bank.

They all laughed and Bernie asked Gerry, "So what are you doing here on a Sunday, Doc?"

"People do get sick on Sundays too, ya' know."

"You still haven't answered my question," Bernie countered as he rolled the dice and landed on one of Jenny's properties. "Damn.''

"You mean I can't stop by to visit on weekends and holidays?"

Jenny interrupted their bantering. "Okay, you guys, cut it out. And Bernie, what kind of host are you? Aren't you going to ask poor Gerry to sit down?"

Bernie smiled and said, "You're right, honey. Say, 'poor Gerry', wanna sit down?"

As Gerry pulled a chair over and sat down, Jenny offered, "Would anyone care for some liquid refreshment? We have lemonade, grape soda, iced tea or diet Pepsi."

Bernie and Gerry winced with distaste, "We'll pass, thanks."

They were all quiet for a moment, and then Bernie said casually, "As a matter of fact, I'm glad you did stop by, pal. There's something I've..." he glanced at Jenny, "I mean 'we' have been meaning to discuss with you."

"Really? Don't tell me you're asking for my consent?" Gerry began smugly.

"No..." Bernie's tone of voice immediately brought Gerry down to a serious mood. "It's about some strange dreams we've been having lately."

"We?"

"Well, it seems Jenny had some dreams while I was in cryogenic suspension that we believe may have very interesting significance."

"Such as?" Gerry asked, slowly, feeling the excitement growing within him.

This time Jenny answered, "The most relevant dream involved Bernie's 'presence' alongside me in bed as I slept." She tried to read Gerry's serious face, to no avail. Bernie nodded for her to continue.

"I opened my eyes to see him there, reaching out to touch my face. I said aloud, 'I love you'; then, as I began to realize the impossibility of his being there, I gasped and sat up abruptly and he ... or whatever 'it' was ... vanished."

"And you don't think it was a dream?" Gerry asked gently.

"Possibly part of one, but as I told Bernie, of one thing I am sure. And that is of his presence in some form that night in my bed." She looked tenderly into Bernie's eyes and smiled knowingly. "I wouldn't mistake that loving feeling anywhere."

Bernie put his arm around her reassuringly and added matter-of-factly, "Besides, if it was a dream, I had the exact same one -- and I don't know for sure -- but it may have been simultaneous ... if you get our drift..."

Gerry remained noncommittally silent for several moments and then stood up and walked to the window, clasping his hands behind him as he stared into the courtyard.

"If it's any help," Bernie offered, "I didn't recall the 'experience' until Jenny began to describe hers ... then it was like an instant playback. I didn't even hear what she was saying. But I can assure you that I also felt the definite sensation of love and warmth that Jenny described at the time of her experience. So that's why we both believe it really happened."

Gerry turned around abruptly. "What really happened?"

Jenny leaned over to kiss Bernie softly on the cheek and then answered, "I think Bernie -- or let's say his 'Soul' -- was really with me that night."

After a moment, Gerry again seated himself across from them and said, "I think you should tell me about any other dreams either one ... or both ... of you has had."

Bernie and Jenny each described their subsequent 'dream' experiences, Jenny with her large group of people transforming into a meeting with Bernie in his den, although he didn't recognize her as 'Jenny'; and Bernie showed Gerry his notes on the dream he had recorded recently also taking place in his den with an unidentified woman.

After listening intently to their experiences, Gerry shook his head in disbelief.

"This could really be 'something'...or ... it could be purely coincidence." He looked at their disappointed faces and smiled, "In any case, you've come to the right person. If anyone can find a shred of significance in all this, I can."

He stood and walked towards the door. "What I'd like you both to do is find some time as soon as possible to record every bit of information you can remember about these experiences, and then I'll sit down and pour over the possibilities and get back to you, okay?"

"Fine with me," Bernie answered.

"Me too, Gerry -- and thanks for lending an ear to two strange people." Jenny added shyly.

"That's the only kind I deal with." Gerry called over his shoulder as he swung the door shut behind him.

Harry fumbled with the keys on his key ring, finally finding the house key to open the door. He swung his jacket over the couch and called out loudly towards the kitchen.

"Marion! Hey -- I'm home."

He walked over to his favorite chair and unfolded the evening's paper to the sports section, then yelled again, getting slightly irritated at his wife's non-appearance.

"Marion! For Chris'sakes, can't ya' at least bring me a beer in here?"

He flipped the page to the football scores. Suddenly, he noticed the silence all around him -- no pans clanking or dishes banging in the kitchen, no vacuum running in the bedroom. "Where the hell is she?" he swore silently, as he pulled himself sluggishly up from the chair and walked to the kitchen.

The large white piece of paper propped up on the kitchen table immediately caught his attention. In her delicately elongated script, Marion had written,

"Dear Harry,

Please believe that I have spent many, many hours thinking about what I must tell you.

The Lord guided me and I now know that it is best if we separate, and maybe even divorce.

I'm sorry I couldn't tell you this in person, but we never were good at talking, Harry.

P.S. I've taken my things and we can settle on the furniture later, although I'd like to keep my grandmother's coffee table, if it's o.k. with you." Marion

Harry realized his hand was shaking as the words blurred before him. He laid the paper down carefully, pulling out a chair to sit on.

Gone. She was really gone. And all she wanted was the damn coffee table.

All of a sudden the whole thing hit him and he found himself crying like a baby, hid head in his arms. Crying -- for the first time since Danny died.

Moments later his sobs began to subside, and he realized first he had lost Danny... and now Marion. He'd lost everything he ever really cared about. He grabbed the note and shoved it in his pocket, then walked to the living room and took his jacket, not knowing where he was going, only that he had to find her.

As he steered his unlit cab down Western Blvd., his mind was racing with confused thoughts and memories from the past. He wondered where Marion had gone and worried about her safety -- she had never been out like this on her own before.

Before he knew it, he was approaching the Clinic. On the spur of the moment, he pulled in the driveway and parked behind the other cabs on duty that night.

He sat there thinking for a moment, then glanced at his watch -- 6:45. Would Bernie be busy? Would he even be able to see him?

"So there you are. I was just going to see if the staff was hassling you or something. Come on in -- I can't tell you how great it is to see you."

He led Harry over to a pair of chairs where they sat down, facing each other.

"Listen, Harry, I want to apologize for not calling you..." Bernie began sincerely, "I've been so darned busy since I checked into this place, I honestly think I'll need a vacation after I get out for some rest and relaxation."

They laughed together and Harry felt a little more comfortable.

"Yeah, that's always the way it is -- all those tests and everything -- especially a special guy like you. They must be having a field day."

"Just about. But I should be getting out this week if all goes well, so you can plan on my inviting me over for another one of Marion's delicious home-cooked meals real soon."

At the mention of Marion, Harry's face clouded with emotion. Bernie spoke softly, sensing the reason his friend was here was not totally social.

"Harry, hey pal ... what is it?"

After a moment, Harry blurted out, "It's Marion. She's gone."

"Gone? What do you mean 'gone'?" Bernie asked excitedly.

"I came home tonight and found this..." he handed Bernie the crumpled note.

Bernie read it quickly and gave it back to Harry. "Oh, Harry... I'm really sorry. Do you have any idea why she left?"

Harry sighed heavily and replied truthfully, "Well, I guess you know as well as I do that we didn't have much of a marriage... not since Danny died. Now that I think back over the years, we both seemed to go our separate ways."

He stood and began pacing back and forth, with Bernie listening quietly.

"I admit I never really thought much about it... I mean, I never really tried to change the way we lived -- until today, and now Marion's done it for me."

He was talking uncontrollably now, letting out all the feelings and thoughts he never expressed to his wife.

"She's a great woman, Bernie. I know that now -- Hell, I've always known it. I was just too damn bullheaded to show any appreciation -- not to mention a bit of affection. Ha! That's a good one. Affection!"

He paced back and forth, shaking his head in anger. "Every time she'd try to get near me I'd tell her to get lost and not interrupt the baseball game on TV or whatever. I guess the truth is, I've just plain forgotten what it's like to enjoy life, Bernie. And now I've driven away my only other reason for living."

He sank back down into the chair, the sobs again racking his body as he held his head in his hands.

Bernie waited patiently for the much-needed tears to subside before speaking. "Harry, I want you to know I feel very close to you and Marion, even though we've only been friends a short time."

Harry looked up and nodded, pulling out his handkerchief to blow his nose.

Bernie mused, "I guess what has happened to me recently has helped me to have a different ... more 'basic' outlook on life. That must be why it's relatively simple for me to see that the root of your problem lies in the beliefs you carry about your son's death."

"What? How?" Harry asked, the shock showing clearly on his face.

"Well, you have to admit that both you and Marion are still grieving to this very day about Danny's death."

'What do you expect us to do? Forget he ever existed?"

"Hold on a minute, now. You also just said you've forgotten what it's like to enjoy life, right?

"Yeah, but..."

"But nothing, Harry. It's time you both realized what a wonderful life you two could be sharing together. Like the saying goes, 'Today is the first day of the rest of your life'," Bernie continued, slowly, "You see, I'm sure you both misunderstand the meaning of 'death'. I ought to know -- I died and am here to tell about it."

Harry listened, a little uncertain of the conversation to follow.

"Have you ever read the Bible?" Bernie asked suddenly.

"Well, no... not really, although my ol' man made me go to Catechism every Sunday as a kid."

"Well, you may recall that it says when one dies he is merely being reborn into the universal realm of the Lord -- a far more appealing place than this earth we inhabit, I'll wager."

"I'm... not sure... I understand..." Harry stammered.

"Well, look at it this way, if you both had been able to 'accept' your son's death as a passage into a much more beautiful and peaceful existence, wouldn't that outlook have changed your subsequent lives together? I mean, you still would have been extremely saddened as one should if their best friend or closest relative was moving permanently to the East Indies or some faraway place. But if it pleased that friend or relative to go there, you would eventually accept their new happiness, even if you couldn't see them every day."

The room filled with silence as both men contemplated their innermost thoughts. Finally, Harry admitted, "Yes, I suppose you're right. But do you think it would help now if we changed our outlook on Danny's death?"

Bernie smiled and said sincerely, "It couldn't hurt."

"Really ... you think so?" Harry asked, sounding like a child begging for confidence.

"Yes ... yes, I certainly do. Now -- do you know where Marion is?"

Harry's smile faded as he realized he had no idea where she was. The only place he could think of was..."Of course! The church. That's it. She has to be there!"

He stood up and shook Bernie's hand vigorously. "Thank you. I can't tell you how great I feel. And I'm sure Danny" and he looked up towards the ceiling "wherever he is ... will be glad to see his ol' pop smiling again after all these years. Be sure to stop by for dinner now -- although I may surprise the little woman and take you both out for dinner instead. Or maybe I'll even cook dinner sometime. I used to fix a great spaghetti and meatballs in my days as a bachelor."

Bernie followed Harry into the corridor and waved, adding, "Don't threaten me or I'll have to bring my bottle of Alka Seltzer!"

Harry laughed and rounded the corner. Bernie walked slowly back to his room, a nagging thought lingering slightly untouchable at the edge of his subconscious. Something about a cure for cancer...

Finally, the thought slipped completely out of reach and he sighed and strolled through the door to his room where he undressed and prepared to take a long, hot bath before retiring for the night.

Marion was sitting in the third pew on the right, with only a handful of other people kneeling in prayer in various places around her. She didn't notice the man who quietly knelt down beside her as she repeated the Lord's prayer once more, this time for Harry.

Softly, the voice from beside her whispered solemnly "And please forgive me, Lord, for all the years of misery I've given my wonderful wife. Now I know why I acted so bad, and I ask your help to make her understand and believe I love her more than anything in the world..."

The tears streaming freely down her face, Marion turned to fall into Harry's loving embrace as he added, "Thank you, Lord, thank you!"

CHAPTER TEN

Gerry had listened intently to the tapes Bernie and Jenny had recorded and had talked to them individually to gain further information. He was in his study at home and it was nearing midnight when he heard the soft knock at the door as his wife walked in.

"Hi honey," she said softly.

"Hi. I thought you'd be asleep by now."

"You know I can't sleep without you." She came up behind him and started to massage the tense muscles in his neck and shoulders.

"Mmm... keep that up and I'll fall asleep right here," he murmured softly as her touch released his tension.

"What are you working on, anyway?" she asked lightly, letting her fingers roam slightly lower and around his chest.

"I forgot." He answered as he moaned lightly in pleasure.

She slapped him playfully on the back and said "Come on! Give!"

Gerry stood up and stretched, feeling the ache from sitting so long. "It's some tapes I had Bernie and Jenny record. It seems they've been having some dreams that may be related to one another and I've been doing a little research on the possibilities, that's all."

"That's all. You wouldn't be spending this much time on it if it was really that simple."

He put his arm around her and led her casually towards the door.

"Listen lady, I haven't come to any astounding conclusions yet, but when and if I do, you'll be the third to know."

She stopped in mid-step and echoed "Third?"

"Well, Bernie and Jenny are entitled to a little priority, don't you think?"

They laughed and kissed each other affectionately, then headed up the stairs to the bedroom.

Gerry left a message for Jenny asking her to let him know when she had some free time so she, Bernie and he could get together for a talk. She called and told him she could spend an hour or so around 1:00 that afternoon, so Gerry arranged the meeting for that time in Bernie's room.

When she got there, Bernie and Gerry were already winding the tapes, starting with hers, so she wouldn't miss anything. She smiled at them both and sat down quietly, and they listened intently.

At the end, Gerry turned off the machine, and stood and began pacing slowly across the room as he spoke.

"As you know, so far we have no evidence of anything supernatural about your dual experiences. I've decided to ask for your cooperation in doing some specific exercises fully monitored and documented in the lab. Are you willing?"

He glanced at Bernie and then Jenny, both of them nodding their agreement to continue.

"Great. Here's what I have in mind. We'll hook you both up to the electroencephalograph when you go to sleep. By the way, Jenny, this will mean your sleeping in the lab a couple of nights..."

She shrugged her shoulders and answered, "No problem."

"Good. Anyway, we'll wake you both up simultaneously after a dream sequence has occurred to record your instantaneous recollection of your dreams. You'll be in separate rooms, of course, to avoid collaboration."

"Aw, you take all the fun out of it," Bernie quipped. "Here I had a king size water bed in mind..."

They all laughed, as Gerry shook his head, adding playfully, "You just can't control yourself, huh, fella? The rumor is already all over the hospital that you didn't waste too much time after your operation." He winked at Jenny, who was turning a bright shade of pink at his statement.

"Okay, you win already," Bernie held up his hands in submission. "Tell us what you hope to accomplish by all this nighttime homework."

"I'm not sure, to tell you the truth. But I think it's a stepping stone towards our advanced understanding of the possibility of dual dreaming and it's significance.

"I know it all means something somehow," Jenny said seriously. "It's just too hard to believe all these things are merely coincidental and timed perfectly with the onset of Bernie's suspended state. In fact, I never remembered <u>any</u> of my dreams before then."

"I know Jenny. That's why we're willing to spend the time and money to see it through," Gerry said as he picked up the tape recorder and headed for the door.

Bernie interjected, "Maybe we'll prove your 'life after death' theory yet, pal."

Gerry stopped at Bernie's words and turned to regard his friend somberly.

"If we do, I'll be eternally grateful to the two of you... and I mean *'eternally'.*" He smiled and waved goodbye to his two good friends, riding high on his intuitive feeling of a great accomplishment about to be made.

Bernie and Jenny had finally fallen to sleep under their slightly uncomfortable arrangement of being wired to various equipment in order to monitor their brain waves and rapid eye movements (REM).

They both started dreaming after about twenty minutes, and Gerry and his technicians watched anxiously for the right moment to trigger the wakeup procedures.

"Good evening, Rosamond."

"Hello." He regarded the lovely lady on the couch much more passively now since they'd been meeting for quite some time.

"Things are progressing well, I see" Electra said as she flipped through a book an archaeology.

"Yes ... I thought you might be pleased. But I'm a little concerned about the outcome of these tests."

"You needn't be. This too has been well prepared in advance.'

She yawned casually and tucked her stocking feet up under her comfortably.

"Well, I'm glad somebody knows what's going on. I don't see why I can never remember the content of our conversations or who you are when I'm awake."

"Perhaps you will ... perhaps you will..." Her form began to fade rapidly and the den with her as a loud voice repeated in his ear,

"Wake up, Bernie. Wake up!"

He opened his eyes groggily to see Gerry standing over him, smiling broadly.

"Let's hear it. Everything you can remember."

"I ... was in my den talking to the same woman ... I can't think of her name, but it was something strange... and we were discussing...I think... these tests… Probably because I was overly aware of them being conducted..."

"Please don't stop to try to evaluate these dreams of yours -- leave that to us. Now go on and just describe what happened in as much detail as possible."

"Well, like I say, we were talking about these tests, and I remember feeling concerned...but she wasn't... and ... well, that's about it, since you woke me up right in the middle of it," Bernie scolded lightly.

"You were about to end the dream anyway and we wanted the impression fresh on your mind. Now be a good boy and go back to sleep so we can monitor the rest of your dreams. Night, night."

Bernie sneered at him and closed his eyes, trying to relax enough to go back to sleep.

Gerry walked to the other room where Jenny's dream remembrance was also being recorded. After she finished, Gerry told her also to go back to sleep and slipped into the lab to listen to her description of her dream.

The tape began, "I had my usual dream with the group of people around me ... only this time I remember a feeling of receiving instructions of some sort... but I can't say what exactly... then I lapsed into the part where I meet with Bernie in his den, and I remember ... well, he seemed tense or worried about something ... whatever it was didn't bother me though -- like I knew somehow everything would be worked out..."

She had paused a moment and Gerry waited to see if she remembered any more of her dreams.

"I don't know why, but I keep thinking of the word 'Electra' ... whatever that means ... and something else like 'Rose'...I can't quite figure out why... sorry -- I guess that's it."

Gerry felt his pulse racing in anticipation as he walked briskly over to the monitors where it appeared Bernie and Jenny were again entering the dream state.

This time their dreams were slightly longer in duration than the first ones.

'Jenny... I mean... Electra? Is there a reason for your assuming Jenny's appearance?'

Electra smiled, playing upon Jenny's innocent features to heighten the effect. "I thought you'd prefer it since you've learned that we are one and the same."

Bernie walked up closer to her, studying every detail as if hoping to find some minute flaw in her 'reconstruction', as it were.

"I don't see why you bother, Rosamond. After all, you must realize everything you see is a product of your own mind, not mine. In fact," she smiled serenely, "I usually prefer to see you as a much taller fellow -- and blond with blue eyes."

"Thanks a lot." Bernie replied testily. "Jenny would never say something like that!"

"Ah... but she just did. You can't blame a person for fantasizing..."

Electra laughed gaily and twirled lightly; landing delicately on the overstuffed sofa before him.

As Bernie brooded, Electra changed back to the more familiar woman's figure and he commented, "That's better. I prefer to keep my interaction with Jenny in the physical state."

"Yes, I can understand your feelings. After all, you are rather limited in your capability to comprehend what you are experiencing now," She taunted him purposely.

"What do you mean by that?" Bernie asked with the intended reaction to her attitude.

"Just that it's really not necessary for you to 'strain' yourself, Rosamond. Although I must admit we did have 'higher hopes', as they say, for your performance."

Bernie sighed heavily. "Just what is it I'm supposed to do to satisfy you people?"

"Wake up."

"What?"

"Wake up Bernie."

"I wasn't through dreaming -- go away." Bernie answered grouchily, waving his arm at Gerry.

"Come on pal ... I know it's hard, but you have to tell me what you were dreaming." Gerry insisted.

Bernie opened his eyes, shaking his head from side to side.

"If you'd ever let me get through one of them, maybe we could get some real information." He took a deep breath, then said, "I was back in my den ... but this time Jenny herself was there. At least in the beginning - then she changed back to the other woman..."

"Electra?" asked Gerry tentatively.

"Yeah. That's the name. How'd you know that?"

"Never mind -- just tell me anything else you remember about your dream."

"Well, I remember I didn't like this Electra posing as Jenny, so I think that's why she changed."

"Any more?"

"Just that I was feeling a little depressed when you woke me up -- something that Electra was saying to me -- but I don't recall what."

"It's okay Bernie. Don't try to remember too hard -- it usually only serves to stimulate your imagination and confuse your actual dream sequence."

"Okay.

The strain of his interrupted sleep was now showing visibly on Bernie's features, so Gerry said, "I think we've accomplished enough for tonight, Bernie. I'll give you a mild sedative so you'll get some sound sleep the rest of the night."

"Whatever you say, Doc" Bernie yawned tiredly.

After seeing Bernie comfortably tucked into his own bed, Gerry raced back to the lab to check on Jenny. She was sitting up, relating the last of her dream story to one of his assistants when she saw Gerry enter the room.

"That's about it," she told the technician.

Gerry signaled for him to leave and transcribe the tapes as he pulled up a chair to sit next to Jenny.

"The same dream?" he asked.

"Yes ... almost... the only difference was that Bernie finally recognized me. How about that?" She laughed and then suddenly turned pensive, "But only at first, then he acted like I was someone else again..."

"Electra perhaps?"

"Electra? You mean that's my name in the dream? I'm not sure, Gerry... I'm sorry, but I just can't say for sure."

"That's okay, Jenny." He patted her hand affectionately. "I think we've established quite a bit tonight."

It didn't matter -- he knew he had to talk to somebody. No, not just anybody -- somebody who cared -- Bernie.

He was afraid to ask the receptionist where Bernie's room was, since he had read in the papers that no one was allowed to see him. As he walked slowly through the busy lobby, an idea began to take form. He headed for the house phone, remembering the name of Bernie's doctor from the news. Disguising his voice as best he could, he told the operator, "This is Dr. Silver -- would you ring Dr. White for me, please? I'm on my way out and had one more thing to tell him."

"Yes doctor," the voice answered politely.

Harry smiled to himself as he saw his plan had worked -- if only Bernie would answer and not someone else.

"Hello?"

The sound of Bernie's familiar voice rang clearly from the other end.

"Bernie? It's Harry Kirby. Am I glad to hear your voice."

"What? Harry? Harry, you ol' dog! How'd you manage to get through to me?"

"If you'll tell me what room you're in, I'll tell you in person. I'm in the lobby now..

"Sure. I'm on the fifth floor. Go left from the elevator and then to the right to 502. Just act like you know where you're going and no one will question you."

"I'll be right up."

Bernie had been right. Harry went unnoticed, quickly locating room 502. He had begun to feel a little nervous about barging in like this, and was about to turn around and leave when Bernie opened his door.

"We have? Really?" she asked excitedly.

"I think so," he repeated. "Now, I've given Bernie a sendative to get some 'restful' sleep and I want you to do the same. Okay?"

"Okay -- I guess I better if I'm going to make my rounds tomorrow."

"Goodnight, Jenny... and thanks."

"Thank you Gerry."

They waved goodbye to each other and Gerry left her to dismiss the other technicians and pick up the tapes. He had told Charlotte he was spending the night there, since he knew he would be up half the night with these tests.

He unlocked his office door and headed for the cot he kept for these occasions, stopping at his desk to insert the tapes in the recorder to play back the night's findings.

As the last of the tapes came to an end, Gerry closed his eyes and drifted into a peaceful slumber, an unusually broad smile spread across his face.

The next night Bernie and Jenny were again wired and taped in order to be monitored by Gerry and his team. They sat waiting patiently for the dials to register a dream starting.

"Good evening, Rosamond."

"Good evening, Electra." Bernie chose good-naturedly to be equally formal in his introduction.

The silence hung almost oppressively around them until, finally, Bernie spoke, "I've been very troubled since we last spoke..." he hesitated, moving across the room to sit at his desk. "I realize now how easy it is for the conscious mind to manifest itself by sheer indoctrination -- even in the 'dream' state."

Electra made no motion or indication she either agreed or disagreed.

Bernie continued, slowly. "I have learned that 'we create our own reality'..." and as he said this his vision seemed to blur inexplicably, but he went on. "And as a result I must teach my conscious self to accept life as such ... merely a recognition of your own desired reality..."

As he paused to ponder the wisdom of the words he had just unwittingly spoken, the room and furnishings around him slowly dissolved, with a sweeping panorama of a beautiful sunset upon a tropical ocean rapidly taking form. As he viewed the unimaginable beautiful colors blending before him, Bernie suddenly, unbelievably, grasped the true meaning of all existence.

He seemed lifted to another dimension where the elevation made all thoughts appear much clearer and more concise. He reveled in the realization that upon reaching this plateau, after all the physical and mental struggles, one finally achieves the simplistic inner peace that we all are born with -

And that was the sum of the lesson ...

Bernie awoke to see the smiling face of Gerry hovering over him. He glanced at the clock and was surprised to see it was already 6:30 a.m.

"So my dream boy finks out on me, eh?" Gerry asked pointedly.

"What?" Bernie struggled to wake up completely, rubbing his eyes with his knuckles.

"Okay -- I suppose you deserved a full night's sleep after last night... but no dreams at all?"

Bernie chose to ignore the question and asked, casually yawning to one side, "Did Jenny dream anything last night?"

"Nope," Gerry answered, "You guys are unbelievable. One night you hardly hit the sack before registering REM activity... and the next night... nothing."

"Sorry Gerry. Have you gotten something out of all this?"

"Oh boy, have I. Listen pal, you may not know it, but you two are the very first documented case of simultaneous dreams – or 'dual dreaming' ever recorded. Not to mention the fact that this only starrted after your much-reported 'death' experience."

They were both silent for a moment and then Bernie said, "Well, I'm just happy I was able to further your research at all, and you know if I can be of any further help..."

"Thanks, but not just yet. I think it's about time we let you out of here to go home to recuperate. I have a feeling you will be well cared for." Gerry smiled knowingly.

"I admit it'll be great to be home for a change. And, to be truthful, Gerry, I can hardly wait to stand in that den of mine -just out of curiosity..."

"I don't blame you -- I'd feel the same way. And just so you won't get bored, I'll give you some correspondence to catch up on." At that, Gerry stepped out into the hall for a moment and returned carrying a large laundry bag stuffed full of letters addressed to Bernie.

"You've got to be kidding." Bernie gasped as he eyed the bulging sack.

Gerry was laughing as he answered, "It's no joke -- you're a very popular guy now. I'm sure this is only the beginning, too."

Bernie groaned and muttered something about having to hire a secretary as he turned to swing out of bed. Gerry clapped him on the back good-naturedly on his way out the door. After Gerry left, Bernie called and left a message for Jenny to stop by as soon as she had time.

"So, the 'man of the hour' finally gets to go home, eh?"

He smiled at her, folding a pair of pajamas neatly and placing them in his suitcase. "Yes, as they say, 'all good things must come to an end'."

"What do you mean by that?" she asked incredulously.

"Oh, I don't know, just no more sneaking around in the Intensive Care Ward, you know -- 'that' sort of thing."

He laughed easily and she was forced to join in, moving into his open embrace eagerly, as he showered her with kisses.

"About the king-sized waterbed..." he teased.

"Never mind -- I'll settle for the double feather-laid bed at your place any time," Jenny answered, seductively pushing him back towards the wall.

"My place at 8:00?" he asked simply.

"I'll be there."

Moments after she arrived, Bernie ushered Jenny immediately into his den where he had just started a large, sputtering fire in the fireplace.

He poured her a glass of port and they sat together on the pair of matching sofas adjacent to the fireplace.

Jenny was the first to speak.

"Did you dream anything last night?"

"Yes, did you?" He somehow knew her answer already.

"Yes." She smiled knowingly,

Again they remained silent for several moments until Jenny again asked, "Why?"

"Hmm?" Bernie seemed lost in his own thoughts.

"Why didn't you tell Gerry about your dream or dreams, if they happened?"

"Because they didn't show up on the monitor" he answered simply. "Why didn't you say something?"

She paused thoughtfully, and then replied, "For the same reason, I guess ... actually, I wanted to talk to you first -- after all, it is sort of a 'personal' matter, don't you think?"

"Exactly," Bernie agreed, and raising her chin, he kissed her lovingly on the lips, both of them lingering on the deep waves of love flowing between them.

They spent the next hour quietly discussing their dual-dreams and openly speculating on the significance of it all.

"Just think," Jenny said with awe in her voice, "to know we live in two different realms simultaneously..."

Bernie nodded, then added, "And the nonphysical one is so vast -- the possibilities seem infinite. It always overwhelms me to try and put what we've experienced into terms others in our physical reality would understand."

"I know what you mean, my love," she agreed comfortingly. "Perhaps we should only 'use' this new information as best we can to help others rather than try to publicize it. After all, I'm afraid the majority of people would never believe us anyway..."

"I think you're right," Bernie laughed suddenly. "They'd probably say my death experience left me minus some marbles upon my return."

They were silent for several more moments, with Bernie thinking of the many people he already planned to help with his newfound knowledge. He knew it wouldn't be easy, but felt he could eventually convince them and aid them in getting in touch with their 'other selves.' At least it was a beginning, he thought to himself. And he planned to continue helping others as long as he remained in this physical state.

Suddenly, Jenny spoke again, "You know, its too bad people are so narrow-minded. After all, what we've experienced corresponds directly with all the ESP and psychic phenomena that's been occurring for years and years."

"Throughout all of history, actually, if people would only recognize it." Bernie put in thoughtfully.

"Yes -- and yet so many remain unconvinced as to the existence of any other realm but the physical." She giggled playfully as she said, "If they only knew that we actually 'create' our own physical reality!"

Bernie joined in her infectious laughter, then pondered aloud more seriously, "Suppose people eventually did believe in what we've learned ... think what a dramatic difference it would make to mankind..."

Their minds simultaneously pictured a different way of life -- one where universal knowledge was accepted and used in daily life. Where the poor and unfortunate of the world could all benefit and improve themselves by tapping this wealth of information. Such a capacity for change existed that inevitably all wars and greed among men would disappear, to be replaced with higher understanding and a consuming need to progress up the infinite ladder of learning.

They were staring into each other's eyes meaningfully, beginning to explore each other in order to complete the mental union they had already achieved, when the phone started to ring obtrusively.

After four rings, Bernie picked up the receiver impatiently, and answered "Hello?"

"Hello? Dr. Bernard White?"

"This is he."

"Maynard Stevens here, sir. I'm with Newman-Strauss Publishing Company in New York. We were wondering if you might be interested in writing a book about your ... well ... your 'death' experience, sir."

Bernie turned to gaze at Jenny momentarily and then answered "I would love to ... but ... I'm afraid no one would ever believe it..." As he hung up the phone, he met Jenny's knowing look with a shrug of his shoulders and led her over to gaze out the window at their mental creation of a beautiful skyline stretching infinitely into the horizon.

THE END

(or is it really the beginning?)

Also Available From Summerland Publishing

Jolinda Pizzirani, author of "Soul Survivor" and the "Psychic Princess" series, takes us into her meditative realm and offers inspirational messages to all who seek Universal knowledge in this life. *"Inspirations"* is a collection of metaphysical poetry that will touch your heart and stir your soul. These verses speak to the theme of Universal Oneness, spiritual salvation and living your physical life to the fullest while in this realm. Open your mind, escape to silence, read and contemplate.

U. S. $8.95 / CAN. $13.00   ISBN: 0-9794585-1-X

Jolinda Pizzirani now brings us this unique collection of messages directly from the angels for all of us to ponder. Every physical entity can hear angel words, but as a prerequisite they must be open to receiving these messages and of a nature to handle and share them properly. Therefore, Jolinda is merely the transcriptionist in this endeavor, and it is hoped that the material provided within "angel words" will begin to satisfy the hunger you have within you for the many unknown factors abundant in Heaven and on Earth.

"angel words" presents a discussion of subjects suggested by the angels themselves, and in addition answers questions submitted by interested individuals living on Earth today. Future editions of "angel words" will embrace the questions put forth by the readers of this first book, and we will continue until all uncertainties have been calmed. Perhaps, as we travel this journey together, we may begin to more successfully navigate the path that lies ahead. U. S. $14.95 / CAN $19.95   ISBN: 0-9794585-3-6

Order from:
www.summerlandpublishing.com, www.barnesandnoble.com,
www.amazon.com, or find it in your favorite bookstore!
Email SummerlandPubs@aol.com for more information.
Summerland Publishing, P. O. Box 493, Summerland, CA 93067